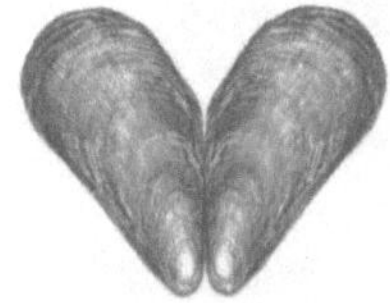

When do hummers dream?

Miranda Jones has made a bold move.
With a promising artist career under way and a lovely home in San Francisco, she has pulled up stakes and moved to a small, coastal town four hours south. Her parents are hurt and disappointed; her sister is worried; and her representative is considering dropping her as a client.

But something feels alive in her new home—something that feeds her soul and nurtures her heart. Is the peace and harmony of her new location short-lived? Does this new-found balance come at the expense of a solid livelihood? Has she retreated from reality only to live in a world of dreams?

Milford-Haven spoke to her the moment she arrived.
A small watercolor she'd painted from imagination bears a striking resemblance to a real location she happens to see during a coastal drive, inspiring her to investigate the sweet little town along the Central Coast. She makes new friends surprisingly fast. The real shock happens when she's suddenly commissioned to paint a mural in the little town. But it's with the rescue of a tiny bird that her works takes on new purpose and her heart knows it's home.

Love or career? Can both be part of her new life?
Friendships abound in Miranda's life, even in her brand new home town. But while her sister dates fascinating men and friends are creating happy marriages, Miranda can only imagine the possibility of romance.

Her family worries that she lives in a world all her own, so rarified and now further isolated, that she'll never find a partner with whom she can share her life. And if she tells them about the uncanny communication she establishes with a hummingbird, they'd suggest she get some "help."

What does new level of intuition signify? How will it affect her painting career? Where else will this ability surface? Is she getting trapped in dreams, or is this the next level of a true awakening?

Come discover what happens … ***When Hummers Dream.***

"...in Mara Purl's enchanting novel *What the Heart Knows*...although the picturesque, seaside setting of Milford-Haven plays an important role in the novel, the cast of interesting and eccentric characters is what really draws the reader into the book. Purl skillfully tackles tough environmental issues such as land development and offshore oil drilling through the lives of her characters and the events that unfold. Detailed descriptions of scenic settings, eccentric characters, and tantalizing storylines combine to make this book one that fans of romance will enjoy."
—BookWire

Mara Purl's *What the Heart Knows* is a first class novel by a very talented writer with strong believable characters, a rapid pace delivery of story, and very tight writing that make this novel such a delight to read. I look forward to seeing other titles in this impressive series.
—Gary Roen, Nationally Syndicated Bookreviewer

The *Milford-Haven Novels* Series

"In Mara Purl's books the writing is crisp and clean, the dialogue realistic, the scenes well described. I salute her ingenuity."
—Bob Johnson, Former Managing Editor
The Associated Press

"Mara Purl has a wonderful way with words and images."
—Sam Summerlin
President/Chairman of The New York Times Syndicate

"Every reader who enjoys book series about small town life has a treat to anticipate in...Mara Purl's Milford-Haven Novels."
—Dee Ann Ray, The Clinton Daily News

"Mara Purl's characters have become old friends and I keep expecting one of them to give me a call!" **—Nanci Cone, Ventura Breeze**

"... in a series of romantic novels centered in the fictional California coastal town of Milford-Haven, we meet . . . an intrigu[ing] cast of diverse characters." **—Fred Klein, Santa Barbara News Press**

PRAISE FROM BOOK BLOGGERS

"You can't escape the pull of Milford-Haven, the setting for *Days of Our Lives* actress and award-winning author Mara Purl's enticing new novel What the Heart Knows. This fictional, coastal California town offers a simpler life. My kind of romance, this [is a] juicy, take-me-away-from-it-all read . . . plus, the inviting story makes you think."

—*Charlotte Hill, Boomer Brief*

"Romance, wisdom and mystery are the topics of *What the Heart Knows* by award-winning author Mara Purl and resonate with women readers. . . . [with] a mix of characters you will not forget . . . . this book was well written, drew me in and kept me on the hook."

—*Dad of Divas Book Review*

ENDORSEMENTS FROM OTHER AUTHORS

"Mara Purl is a skillful storyteller who has written a charming and tantalizing saga about the ways in which lives can intersect and be forever changed. The first novel in the saga is not-to-be-missed."

—*Margaret Coel*
New York Times *best-selling author*

"Mara Purl tells stories from the heart. Don't miss her Milford-Haven novels."

—*Kathy (Mrs. Louis) L'Amour*

"Don't read Mara Purl's Milford-Haven series—unless you want to be captivated!"

—*Nichelle Nichols*
Best-Selling Author of "Beyond Uhura–Star Trek Memories"

When Hummers Dream

Also by MARA PURL

Fiction

When the Heart Listens
A Milford-Haven Novella (Prequel)

What the Heart Knows
A Milford-Haven Novel (Book One)

Where the Heart Lives
A Milford-Haven Novel (Book Two)

When Hummers Dream
A Milford-Haven Novelette

When Whales Watch
A Milford-Haven Novella

When Otters Play
A Milford-Haven Novella

Holiday Novelettes & Novellas

Where An Angel's On a Rope

When Angels Paint

Whose Angel Key Ring

Non-Fiction

Act Right:
A Manual for the On-Camera Actor
(with Erin Gray)

Kenneth Leventhal & Co.:
A History of the Firm

S.T.A.R –Student Theatre & Radio
High School Curriculum; College Curriculum

Plays

Mary Shelley–
In Her Own Words
(with Sydney Swire)

Dracula's Last Tour

Screenplays &
Teleplays

The Meridian Factor
(with Verne Nobles)

Welcome to
Milford-Haven
(with Katherine
Doughtie Nolan)

Guiding Light

Radio Plays

Milford-Haven, U.S.A
(100 episodes)

Green Valley

Haven Ten

S.T.A.R.
Teleplay

Only A Test

S.T.A.R.
Radio Plays

America the Beautiful
Ashton Valley
Boom
Caught in a Web
Changes
Cruising
The Curse of
Santa Florida
Deep Freeze
Fountain Hills Mall
Friendz
Frozen Hearts
The Game
Going Somewhere
In or Out
The Journal
K-RAP
Love Child
Love Resolutions
The New Girl
The Peak Mystery
San Feliz
Secretos
Tokyo Time Travel
Toxicity
Westland High
Wrong Way

Mara Purl

When Hummers Dream

A Milford-Haven Novelette

When Hummers Dream ©2011 by Mara Purl
New Edition

www.BellekeepBooks.com

Front Cover – Original Watercolor by Mary Helsaple ©2012
Front, Back Covers and Jacket design by Tara Goff, Bellekeep Books
and Kevin Meyer, Amalgamated Pixels
©2013 by Milford-Haven Enterprises, LLC.
Copy Editor: Vicki Werkley.
Proofreader: Jean Laidig.
Author photos: Lesley Bohm.

Milford-Haven PUBLISHING, RECORDING & BROADCASTING HISTORY
This book is based in part upon the original radio drama Milford-Haven ©1987 by Mara Purl, Library of Congress numbers SR188828, SR190790, SR194010; and upon the original radio drama Milford-Haven, U.S.A. ©1992 by Mara Purl, Library of Congress number SR232-483, broadcast by the British Broadcasting Company's BBC Radio 5 Network, and which is also currently in release in audio formats as Milford-Haven, U.S.A. ©1992 by Mara Purl.
Portions of this material also appear on the Milford-Haven Web Site,
http://www.MilfordHaven.com © by Mara Purl.

Publisher's Cataloging-In-Publication Data
Names: Purl, Mara.
Title: When hummers dream / Mara Purl.
Other Titles: Milford-Haven U.S.A. (Radio program) | Milford-Haven (Radio program)
Description: New York, NY : Bellekeep Books, [2017] | Series: A Milford-Haven novelette ; [bk. 1] | Previously released as an ebook, 2011. | Based in part upon the original radio dramas Milford-Haven and Milford-Haven U.S.A., broadcast by BBC Radio 5 Network.

Identifier: ISBN 9781936878819
Subjects: LCSH: Hummingbirds — California — Fiction.
Bird watching — California — Fiction. | Painters — California — Fiction.
California--Fiction. | LCGFT: Action and adventure fiction.

Published in the U.S. by Bellekeep Books, New York
www.BellekeepBooks.com.

Distributed by Midpoint Trade Books, New York
www.MidpointTrade.com

10   9   8   7   6   5   4   3   2   1

Printed in the United States of America

*This story is dedicated to
the tiny and mighty birds
who migrate thousands of miles each year,
and to those who love them.*

Acknowledgements

The New Edition

Thanks to my publishers: Patrice Samara, Kara Johnson and Tara Goff at BelleKeep Books. Thanks to my gifted editorial team: Vicki Hessel Werkley, editor; Jean Laidig, proofreader. Thanks to Mary Helsaple for exquisite watercolors for my book covers, and to Kevin Meyer and Rebecca Finkel for superb cover design and graphics.

Thanks to my marketing team: Jonatha King at King Communications in Santa Barbara for PR and marketing; Kelly Johnson and Sky Esser for internet design and wizardry.

Thanks to those who provide expertise during my research: to artists Mary Helsaple, Caren Pearson for inspiration and depth of detail.

Thanks to dear friends in Cambria who've supported Milford-Haven for many years with such enthusiasm, including Elaine Traxel Evans, Kathe Tanner, Susan Berry, Simon Wilder, Freedom Barry, and Jim Buckley. Thanks to Verne Nobles for vision and commitment to the Milford-Haven Television project.

Thanks for special events: to dynamic organizations in several parts of the country for working with me to produce the community-based Milford-Haven Socie-Teas® (Possibili-Teas, Generosi-Teas, Hospitali-Teas, Creativi-Teas, and our list continues!) And to Unique Soap Boutique for the wonderful Days Of Our Lives events.

Thanks for organization support: WWW (Women Writing the West), CLAS (California Literary Arts Society), IBPA (Independent Book Publishing Association), PALA (Publishers Association of Los Angeles), and Author U—serving with worthy colleagues on boards and advisory boards has taught me so much and continues to be a privilege.

Thanks to all at Haven Books for helping to create the original platform. Thanks to my mentor Louis L'Amour, who believed in my project and told me to keep going with it.

And most important of all—thanks to you, my readers.

The Radio Drama

Milford-Haven had its first air date in 1987, and my thanks go to KOTR, in Cambria, California, our first radio home. In its next incarnation Milford-Haven, U.S.A. was broadcast on the BBC, thanks Ms. Pat Ewing, Director of Radio 5—a maverick network that launched a maverick show, and celebrated with us when we reached 4.5 million listeners.

Thanks to both the original cast of Milford-Haven and to the cast of Milford-Haven, U.S.A., seasoned professionals who brought my characters so vividly to life that their work is inextricably woven into the fabric of the characters themselves.

Thanks to Engineer Bill Berkuta whose Afterhours Recording Company became our studio home, a workshop in which we created one hundred episodes of the first show and sixty of the second, and where we now create audio books of the novels.

Thanks to Marilyn Harris and Mark Wolfram, who composed the haunting Milford-Haven theme and all the music cues that support the emotional ebb and flow of the story.

Before I created my own soap opera, there was *Days of Our Lives* and my thanks go to the producers, writers, directors and fellow cast members with whom I worked, and from whom I learned so much.

And before there was a Milford-Haven, there was a young woman who had always lived in cities—Tokyo, New York, Los Angeles. I spent a summer performing in a play at Jim and Olga Buckley's Pewter Plough Playhouse in Cambria, and became fascinated with the life in and of a small town. With Elaine Traxel Evans's help, I immersed myself in this new culture— admittedly seeing it through the eyes of an environ-mentalist—and began to realize that it was not only a local drama that was being played out in its quiet streets, but a universal one as well.

Listeners in the U.S. and in the U.K. agreed, writing to me about their own lives, their own towns, and the commonality of the situations we face globally. Several years later the link with listeners was vividly demonstrated, when the original Milford Haven in Wales embraced me as an honorary citizen and showed me those same streets, those same dramas, uncannily alike in the multi-cultural parallel univers-es we all inhabit. Thanks to Bruce Henrickson of the Belhaven House Hotel. Special thanks to Jim and Anne Hughes, who shared my vision even before we met, who welcomed me into their home, and with whom I continue to forge a unique town-to-town relationship.

My thanks go to my family and friends—helpful, discerning and, above all, supportive—Ray Purl, Marshie Purl, Linda Purl, Larry Norfleet, Erin Gray, Miranda Kenrick, Vickie and Bob Zoellner.

And finally my thanks go to my characters, among whom are— Jack, Zack, Miranda, Cornelius, Samantha, Rune, Meredith, Connie, Rick, Emily, Kevin, Joseph, Sally, Tony, Zelda, Notes, Susan and Cynthia, who are building, buying, painting, observing, planning, rehearsing, flirting, traveling, dealing, reporting, cogitating, dominating, dishing, healing, conniving, playing, sneaking and seducing, respectively.

Dear Reader –

Welcome to Milford-Haven! If this is your inaugural visit, it's my pleasure to introduce you to my favorite little town and to a few of its many residents—all of whom are described in the Cast of Characters for the series near the end of the book.

This novelette features artist Miranda Jones, and gives you a glimpse of her new life in a small coastal town. The story stands alone as a complete tale, but is also woven into the overall tapestry of the Milford-Haven saga. Chronologically, *When Hummers Dream* occurs just after the series prequel *When the Heart Listens,* and just before *What the Heart Knows,* book one of the Milford-Haven Novels. Indeed, to give you a seamless transition—and to let you pick up the first thread of the ongoing mystery—you'll find the Prologue and Chapter One of the first novel are waiting for you after the story.

In future novels, we'll travel with Miranda to destinations that fascinate her painter's eye and her restless heart. This novelette takes her—and you—into the unexpectedly magical aspects of her new hometown, and introduces you to new friends, and an irritating visitor.

This brief sojourn to California's glorious Central Coast is a window opening outward to sheer escape, and a window opening inward to pure reflection. For you, it might be either . . . or both!

As this short book unfolds, follow my footsteps over the interconnected pathways of those who inhabit Milford-Haven, and come to that timeless place when even hummingbirds can dream.

Mara Purl

Every great dream begins with a dreamer.
——Harriet Tubman

Spread your wings and let your spirit soar.
—Anonymous

Chapter 1

Miranda Jones, grasping a mug of warm lemon-tea in one hand, with her other hand slid open the door to her deck, grinning at the complex trill of a robin.

She stepped out into the cool freshness just in time to see the first rays of sun arrow over the ridge behind her house, then race through a thick stand of pines to pierce the Pacific waves dancing in the near distance.

After sinking into a deck chair, she was about to sip her tea when something bulleted past her head. She ducked, nearly spilling her drink. She whipped her head around to discover what it was, but saw no silhouette against the pale sky. *Some kind of flying critter . . . nearly penetrated my ear and flew off with a hank of my hair. Well, not really,* she admitted. *But what was that? Too small to be the robin, too large for a bumble bee. A hummingbird? But why? It's not like I had anything sweet nearby . . . no nectar . . . nothing red.*

Leaving the mystery unsolved, she glanced over at the hammock she'd recently added to her deck furniture. *I've been in Milford-Haven for eight months, but I'm still figuring out what works for my new space, still getting settled.* The hammock—a stretched-fabric bed fitted to a metal frame—made her smile. An indulgence . . . but, it seemed perfect right there. *That dark green canvas echoes the living room couch . . . blends with the pines out here. . . . I haven't really tried it out, except just for a minute right after Kevin helped me set it up.*

One of several new friends, Kevin Ransom—a tall, quiet guy she'd met during her first visit to Milford-Haven a few months ago—worked at a local construction company. Known around town as someone who knew how to build, assemble, or wire just about anything, most of all, he was known for helping others. She'd readily accepted his offer to help her install her new hammock, as well as several other items around her new rental house.

I really should try the hammock. A breeze swept across the deck and swirled through the open neck of her fleece. *It's still chilly out. Maybe I should grab my quilt.* She rose and went inside, set her now-cool mug of tea on a living room end table, and grabbed the colorful coverlet draped over the end of the sofa. Returning to the deck, she slid onto the hammock and pulled over her the favorite gift Meredith had special-ordered for her as a moving-away present.

For about a year, she and her sister had been roommates in San Francisco: Meri, the successful financial adviser; Mandy the struggling artist. A few months before that, a top artist's representative, Zelda McIntyre, had "discovered" her, and her paintings began to sell in some of the city's best galleries. Once the siblings were roommates, things hadn't always been harmonious. That'd only inspired Miranda to move forward with her own plans.

Recently, Meri had delivered photos of some of Miranda's landscape paintings to a local craftswoman who offered a unique service: she'd reproduce photographic images onto soft cotton squares, then sew them into quilts. The paintings Meredith had chosen now traced across the fabric like windows into their childhoods: the blues of beach-days; the greens of forest walks; the lavenders of north-coast sunsets. *Something of a peace offering from Meri. Still, I love it!*

Snuggling under the puffy quilt, Miranda sank comfortably back against the pillows to savor the gentle movement of the hammock while her gaze traced the sunrays that bypassed her deck to shatter into diamonds on the surface of the waves.

Love catching these first moments of the day. Gives me a head start. Though her logic-mind might still be half-asleep, her artist-eyes were already at work. *The colors . . . they're never the same. This morning the clouds scudding by are lemon-custard; the sea is teal, where I can see it. And the pines seem soft, as though carved of candle wax.*

But even as she tried to continue cataloguing the details that her painter's eyes couldn't help but notice, her lids began to close as the gentle motion of the hammock lulled her into a early-morning nap.

Miranda heard a faint hissing sound and began walking toward it. Sprinklers, *she thought,* I must be near a garden.

A high hedge climbed in the morning mist and parted in the middle where she moved through, her bare legs tingling from the low, gentle spray of water that misted through the plantings.

In the drenched garden, ferns arced up to her shoulders; thick ivy draped down over a high fence; raised beds dripped with bleeding hearts; and curving pathways swirled with rainbow arrays of impatiens.

I don't see them, but I smell roses. *At a far corner, she glimpsed a charming arched trellis and went toward it for a closer look. She reached out to touch the inch-thick stem of the sturdy plants twined through its lattice, but jerked back her hand when a huge thorn pierced her finger.* Why would there be a thorn? Unless . . . this stem is twenty feet high and two inches thick . . . but it's a rose bush!

A single drop of blood oozed from her fingertip, to fall in slow motion onto the fertile ground. As Miranda continued to watch that spot, a tiny green shoot pushed its way through the soil, climbing steadily upward till it reached her shoulder. Then a bud appeared and opened into a single red rose.

As she leaned to inhale its rich fragrance, a hummingbird raced her for the privilege, pushing his long bill deep into the heart of the flower.

Then the hummer turned to face her, winked, and zoomed past her ear.

Miranda blinked her eyes open with a start. *Was someone just watching me?* She glanced around her deck. *No, of course not. Yet I feel a presence of some kind. Of course I know the local critters are always watching. . . .*

Peeling back the quilt, she threw her legs over the side of the hammock, stood, and stretched. *Wonder how long I napped?* She looked toward the east, noticing the sun now rode higher above the mountains. *Probably an hour, or so. Time to get moving.*

She thought of her plan for the day: to paint the flora and fauna at a favorite spot, the Rosencrantz Café and Guildenstern Garden. The whimsical name—which always made her smile—hinted at the style of the place: part history, part culture, part nature. A lovely redwood-and-glass structure set atop a hill, it overlooked the ocean and was angled to take advantage of the view north toward the Santa Carlita Cove and the Piedras Blancas Lighthouse beyond.

The spacious back yard of the café offered a series of redwood decks surrounded by a garden and its adjoining nursery. The owners Robin and George—who'd used their *R* and *G* to improvise the name—were committed to featuring Central Coast varietals, and were well versed in the history and genus of each plant they carried.

The profusion of indigenous and imported species, the myriad colors and the charming architecture of the garden's paths, fountains and seating areas not only had made the R&G a revelation to tourists who happened by, but also had created a loyal following among local residents.

For a wildlife and landscape artist like Miranda, it provided a research library and laboratory. She'd made arrangements with Lucy, the restaurant manager, to spend six hours in the garden. She'd tried for a day mid-week, but for liability reasons, Robin had suggested the Friday-through-Sunday schedule, when they had more staff. Meanwhile Miranda'd already visited several times, filling pages of her artist-journal with sketches and watercolor studies. *Now I'm ready for a day of painting fully completed pieces.*

She'd need her folding art-table—the one she used in place of an easel when she painted with watercolor—to hold her work level and allow her to control the movement of her liquid colors. And she'd need a hat, brush carrier, as well as small water bottles.

Grabbing the quilt from the hammock, she went inside, draped the coverlet back over the sofa, and walked into her adjacent studio to gather the day's materials.

A few minutes later, with her supplies packed and waiting by her front door, she ran downstairs to shower and dress.

Chapter 2

Lucy Seecor tossed her long, black braid over one shoulder and began to count out the flatware. The bright blue napkins were already laid out, ready to wrap the silver.

"Expecting any larger groups today, Luce?"

Lucy glanced up and watched for a moment as her boss unloaded a carrier tray of glasses. "Just the Ragged Point Book Club ladies. It's their monthly meeting."

"Right. They're a nice group. What time are they booked?"

"Not till one o'clock," Lucy replied, not missing a beat in her work with the silver.

Robin shook his head. "Never can figure out how you keep the whole month's schedule in your brain. Not that I'm complaining!"

Lucy chuckled.

"Anything else going on today?"

"Just Miranda Jones."

"Oh! That's today! I'd forgotten. Anything I need to prepare?"

"Already got it handled," Lucy said.

"Of course you do!" Robin shook his head again. "As always. Okay, then, I'll be in the kitchen."

As Robin left to resume his culinary duties, Lucy paused for a moment, looking out the huge picture window at the spectacular ocean view, so adored by the restaurant patrons.

Miranda Jones . . . so dedicated to her art. Hope I can grab a moment to see how she does it. Always wanted to paint. Never had the time. Well, maybe one day. . . .

Miranda rolled her vintage Mustang to a stop in the graveled parking lot of the R&G Café & Garden. *R&G . . . that's what the regulars call it. Looks like I'm getting here early enough . . . no other cars parked yet.*

She grabbed her watercolor bag and folded table, then entered via the nursery—walking through display aisles of potted plants and small, burbling fountains—until she emerged at the entrance to the garden itself.

Out in the open again, she glanced up at the sky to check the light. *Slight haze . . . nice. It'll act like a giant diffuser.* She looked around at the redwood tables, raised flower beds, winding pathways, and lamp posts with hanging baskets, as she considered the best location for her day's work.

As her gaze rotated across the open space, she paused, captured by an unexpected perfection. Across the garden, a glass wall acted as a windbreak for guests who chose to eat outside. The uprights supporting the glass perfectly framed a view of the ocean. *Well . . . there it is . . . a ready-made painting if I ever saw one.*

She moved forward, watching closely as the visual frame adjusted, then she backed up again, choosing the ideal position. Grinning at the serendipity of the find, she placed her bag on the ground, set up her worktable, and went to look for Lucy.

She opened one of the double glass doors that led inside. On the ground level, a long, polished bar ran along a mirrored wall and small round tables spread across the floor—all deserted till evening. She took the stairs up to the restaurant, pausing as she reached the top to gaze out at the view, even more stunning from this higher level.

"Hi, Miranda." The restaurant manager Lucy approached with a smile, hand outstretched. "Welcome! We've been expecting you."

"Good to see you again, Lucy. I'm really looking forward to this. Can I show you where I was thinking of setting up?"

"Sure." Lucy led the way downstairs and onto the terraced exterior, glimpsing Miranda's table and bag. "Oh, that should be fine."

"I won't be in the way of any of your customers?"

"No. Actually, I think they'll be intrigued." Lucy chuckled. "Who knows, you might become a new tourist attraction!"

"Oh, I hope not!" Miranda tried to hide a grimace. "I'll do my best to be inconspicuous."

"Uh . . . would you mind if. . . ."

"What?" Miranda encouraged.

"Well, I'd love to watch you paint. I mean, I doubt I'll have much time, but if I can sneak away . . . would it bother you?"

"Um, no. You won't bother me."

"Really? Oh, that's great! So, can I bring you anything? A glass of raspberry iced tea?"

Miranda couldn't help but smile at the childlike exuberance, then said, "I'll save that special treat to have with lunch. Well, I think I'll get started before your customers start to arrive."

"Enjoy!" Lucy tossed her long braid over her shoulder, and returned to her duties inside.

Miranda reached down to open her bag. As she pulled out her portable watercolor palette with its small individual pans, her mind automatically cataloged how she'd mix the gradations of color from the few primary shades she kept in her travel kit. She'd squeeze color from the tubes—warm colors on the right, cool on the left.

A loud buzzing whizzed by her ear and she glanced up in time to see a hummingbird speed across the garden at eye level. *So it probably was a hummer that buzzed me this morning! Perfect. He'll be part of my painting today. That's a rufous . . . jewel-bright and aggressive.*

Of the 356 species of hummingbird she'd read about and watched on film in recent years, she knew the rufous migration patterns meant this was their time of year to be on California's Central Coast. In October, the tiny birds winged all the way back to Mexico for the winter.

The iridescence of the species posed a special challenge to making the jewel-tone feathers look realistic, but she knew how to handle it. She always packed her Daniel Smith Luminescent, a special additive that could be mixed into any color, making it appear pearlescent.

Okay, now water and brushes. She rummaged in her bag, pulling out her favorite small water bottle that, when squeezed, pushed out a supply of clean water into a small well on its top. She brought out her selection of brushes: three round—sizes two, four and six—and two flat—sizes two and four.

Next she reviewed the media she'd brought. First were her trusty three-by-five and five-by-seven watercolor blocks— heavy pads of paper from which sheets could later be removed individually. Second were a few differently sized Ampersand

Claybords-for-watermedia—masonite wood panels with their special water-and-paper layers added to one side, ideal for creating small, collectible pieces. *I think I'll start with the smallest Claybords, experiment a bit and get the colors right.* These'd have to sealed, later, with clear acrylic spray so the images wouldn't wash off. That reminded her she'd need her tiny spray water bottle to keep the paint liquid in case it started to dry too fast.

With her portable studio ready, Miranda pulled two more things from her bag—a wide-brimmed folding straw hat, which she popped right onto her head; and one of her three-by-three Claybords. Now she stood quietly, inhaled, then bent her knees and began shifting her weight in a *Tai Chi* brush-knee movement. After a few rotations, she picked up her palette, her number two flat brush, and began to paint.

Chapter 3

Randi Raines looked around the rustic café and pouted. Already the long weekend wasn't panning out to be all she'd hoped. Her boyfriend—if he could really be called that yet—had promised a "romantic getaway" up the coast.

She'd made special arrangements to take both Thursday and Friday off from her high-pressure job as an L.A. radio talk-show host, and she'd pictured someplace glamorous and sophisticated, expensive and well-manicured. For accommodations, she'd imagined a suite at the Ritz Carlton in Santa Barbara. Instead, they'd stayed the night at some two-bit motel in this dumb little town she'd never heard of called Milford-Haven.

For two and a half days, now, Will had *talked* about nothing but how "fantastic" the Central Coast was, and *done* nothing but drag her off to "explore." First, it was a hike into a bunch of trees he'd called a forest. All she'd gotten there was a case of poison oak. Second, it was dinner at some hole-in-the-wall that claimed to be fancy. *In a pig's eye.* In fact, she'd had the pork—refusing to allow them to cook it in the plum sauce they'd recommended—and found it nearly as dry as her date's stories.

Now he'd convinced her they *had* to have lunch at this "magical garden" place. All she saw were redwood tables and benches where she'd probably get a splinter in her tush. *Thank you very much.* And across the garden, sat an artist poking at a piece of paper with a brush. *How quaint.*

Since the rest of their weekend stretched out ahead of her, all she had to look forward to was another boring meal followed by two more days of the same. So she'd decided to drown her sorrows. That was one thing this area of California was known for—wine. She'd ordered a whole bottle of local Chardonnay, and now she was working her way to the bottom of her second glass.

"You'd think a *nice* restaurant like this could afford to paint their tables, right?" Randi giggled, enjoying how Will winced and looked around to see if anyone had heard her comment. *So what if I'm talking loud? He doesn't listen to me anyway!*

They'd ordered a while ago from a cute waitress. *Will looked at her a moment too long. I may not be the hottest Hollywood babe, but I've got a tight body and just had my hair frosted. Think I'll pull my top a little further off my shoulder.* "Say, why is the service so slow here?"

"Randi, the service isn't slow. They're just giving us a chance to enjoy our drinks."

"Oh! Goody!" She giggled again and managed not to stick out her tongue when someone at a nearby table darted a look in her direction.

The cute waitress came back to deliver some pita chips. Randi swiped at the bowl, nearly overturning her wine glass. Will caught it, then set it down carefully, a tiny grimace pinching his expression.

"Nice weekend, Will. Thanks!" Randi took another sip of wine. "Course, in this *secluded* place we'll never manage to see *anybody*. Or be seen by *anybody*, for that matter." She cut loose with a high-pitched laugh. "There's probably not enough *culture* to make anybody important come to this town. Although *we* came here, didn't we?" She slapped the table. "Why *did* we come here anyway? We could still hurry on down to Santa Barbara where the beautiful people are."

"We don't have to go anywhere, Randi."

Not sure what he meant, she asked, "Really?"

"Oh, yeah. All the 'beautiful people' are right at this table."

Not sure whether or not Will had just made a joke at her expense, Randi threw back her head and laughed just the same.

Miranda's hand jerked, an involuntary reaction to the shriek of laughter that'd pierced the air. Since the hand held a paint-saturated brush close to the five-by-eight Claybord she'd started to work on, the movement left a streak of blue as a memorial of the event.

Startled, she had a sudden, brief sensation of hovering above herself, watching her hand, the brush, the painting. For just a moment, fragments of a dream came back to her: something about a garden . . . a hummingbird with its beak in a rose. *Odd, because roses don't have nectar. But the hummer could've been drinking water captured in the petals.* Traces of the dream lingered, but they were burning off as quickly as the marine layer that'd blanketed the shore in the early morning.

The quiet of the garden had been shattered, as had her reverie of work. When she'd chosen the ideal spot to take advantage of the view, she'd been alone in the garden. Now,

Miranda sat on a redwood bench in front of her art-table, closed her eyes and inhaled, then blew air slowly from between pursed lips.

People on vacation . . . they just don't realize how much noise they make. To be expected. August weekends always bring the tourists. She sighed. *Since they're crucial to the economy, I shouldn't complain. In fact, I'm benefitting too, since the gallery that sells my work is doing a brisk business this summer.*

So—obnoxious and oblivious though they could be—these tourists served an important function. They came with their backpacks and leisure suits, their sensible walking shoes and colorful baseball caps. They came with their money. And they came with their noise.

The shrieking woman continued to laugh at her own jokes, her demeanor evidently loosened by too much wine.

I have to admit, Milford-Haven's an ideal spot for a weekend getaway. A good four-hour drive from either Los Angeles or San Francisco, the tiny coastal town remained just slightly beyond convenient reach for most, and that suited her—and all the other residents in town—just fine.

It was a dichotomy, she supposed. On one hand, it was a pristine haven with a core value of privacy and a cherished goal *not* to be found out. But on the other hand, it survived in good measure at the caprice of those who *did* discover the well-kept secret of a jewel at the heart of the Central Coast.

Actually, today's a perfect example. Now that the clouds have lifted, everything looks polished as jewelry. She took a moment to savor the visual treat: ocean spread out below the bluff like a sea of sapphires; bright sun gilded the leaves; hummingbirds winged through the garden like floating emeralds and rubies.

She inhaled, smiled, then looked down at her palette to check her colors. Summer generally suffused a light haze over the landscape, gentling the tonalities and softening all the edges. But now the slight cloud cover had cleared, leaving the air clear as fine crystal, the colors deep and rich.

Miranda squeezed another dot from the tube of Cerulcan Blue Chromium and swirled her brush, tapering it off the edge of her board.

With the sky brighter, now, it's actually perfect having this streak of vivid color across the top of the picture. Let the painting come through, she schooled herself. *It's not really yours anyway.*

Chapter 4

Samantha Hugo headed toward the front door of the Rosencrantz Café, smiling with anticipation. She and her young friend Miranda had agreed to treat themselves today and would soon be enjoying their favorite R&G signature meal: fish-and-chips with red-cabbage slaw.

But if I know Miranda, she's not waiting alone at a table. She's still painting. Better go check the garden. Changing direction, Sam walked through the shade of the nursery entrance, then back out into the sun to glance around the Guildenstern Garden.

Catching sight of Miranda sitting at her worktable, she watched as the artist waved her paintbrush to greet Sam. "Hi!" Sam stepped close enough to catch sight of an array of tiny watercolors, and a nearly-finished book-sized painting of the garden. "Oh, how gorgeous! Look at those colors!"

Miranda stood up and gave Sam a light hug. "Hungry?" she asked.

"Famished. Oh, there's Lorraine having lunch with some friends. Do you mind if I tell her one quick thing?"

"Of course not." Miranda plunged her brush into water. "I need to clean my brushes and close up a bit here."

"Sorry, I won't be a moment." Sam hurried across the garden to greet Lorraine Larimer. Known affectionately as the "crone" of Milford-Haven, Mrs. Larimer served as head of the Town Council and ruled their small burg with the proverbial iron-fist-in-velvet-glove.

"Hi, everybody, hi, Lorraine. Pardon me for interrupting. I just wanted you to know I did find that report I promised I'd look for. Do you want me to drop it by your office, or will you send someone to pick it up?"

"Good as gold—as always, Sam. I'll come get it myself. This afternoon okay?"

"Perfect. I'll be back at my desk by two or so. Enjoy your lunch."

Sam walked toward the back door, Miranda met her there, and the two made their way upstairs, where Sam had reserved their favorite corner table with its ocean view. Lucy greeted them, guided them to their table, and as they were seated asked, "I imagine you ladies know exactly what you want?"

Laughing, Sam gave the order without so much as a glance at the familiar menu.

Smiling, Lucy said, "I'll tell your waitress."

After Lucy left, the two friends sat in silence for a long moment, staring out the wall-to-wall plate glass windows, allowing the sparkles off the Pacific to dance in their eyes.

Samantha murmured, "Glad that earlier marine layer burned off."

"I love it clear like this, but I love the cloud cover too," Miranda confessed. "The colors vibrate under that diffused light." She turned to look at Sam. "Lighting is so important . . . like looking at your hair right now. . . transparent Pyrrole Orange mixed with Quincridone Red Light, with a base color of Primary Magenta. Yup, that'd capture it I think, though no paint could ever do your color justice."

Sam could feel herself blush at the compliment. "That's very kind, Miranda. But you know, these days, it comes just as much from a tube as your paints do."

"Yeah, but I've seen photos. That *was* your natural color. Incredible."

Their waitress brought two tall glasses of iced raspberry tea, and Sam took a sip of hers. *What a sweetheart. If I'd ever had a daughter, she'd be about Miranda's age, and I hope she'd be just like her.*

"Okay, Sam, so catch me up. What's going on in those secret meetings behind closed doors at the Environmental Planning Commission?"

Sam laughed. "I don't know. Every time I think we've got a really good piece of legislation ready to place on the next ballot—something everyone in town could agree on—another objection comes out of left field and blows a hole right through the center of it."

Miranda tossed her long brunette hair back over her shoulder. "What is it this time?"

"A coastal erosion protection measure. Basically, all it says is that houses can't be built right up to the edge of a bluff." Sam took another sip of tea. "I mean, why would anyone want to build that close anyway?"

"Exactly." Miranda nodded. "With the constant erosion, it's not like the location of the bluff is the same now as it was a hundred years ago."

"I'd hate to wake up in the middle of the night wondering if my bed was about to crash over a cliff."

Miranda grimaced. "Nasty thought."

"There's even a provision for older homes, grandfathering them an exemption. We're not asking people to dismantle their houses."

Miranda reflected for a moment. "But they can't necessarily build new decks if their house is already too close to the edge?"

"Right."

Sam saw the waitress bringing their food, the fragrance apparently wafting past other customers whose heads turned in appreciation.

"Here we go," she said cheerfully. "Anything else I can bring you ladies?"

"We're fine for now. Thanks." Sam spread a blue linen napkin across her lap.

Miranda dipped an end of crisp fish into tartar sauce and sank her teeth into the delicate cod. "Mmm," she said, wiping sauce from the edge of her mouth. "I always forget just how terrific this is until I taste it again."

Sam, savoring the excellent slaw, closed her eyes. "Wish I could figure out their secret ingredient," she murmured.

The friends ate in silence for a while, each lost in her own thoughts. Then Sam continued their conversation. "I don't know, Miranda, it feels as if this town is getting more and more polarized. We've got developers versus environmentalists, artists against the construction workers—"

"Against?" Miranda asked. "Well, I don't have anything *against* the construction workers."

"Unless they come along and chop down your favorite tree."

"True," Miranda admitted.

"You know what I mean. This was always a haven for artists, crafts people, folks with a sense of beauty and nature who wanted to keep it that way. Now we're getting a lot of pressure to build and develop, scrape away hillsides and put in shopping centers."

Sam looked up just in time to see Lucy approaching with two more diners—one of them Jack Sawyer. *Oh, no! Of all times . . . of all places!* The last thing she needed was an unscheduled encounter with her primary adversary, the head of Sawyer Construction—a man who also just happened to be her ex-husband, though no one in town other than Miranda knew about their personal relationship.

To make matters worse, she couldn't help but notice he attracted plenty of female attention. Barrel-chested and still as ruggedly handsome as ever, he wore tight jeans poured into work boots that pounded across the floor. As usual, his employee Kevin Ransom followed like a tall, thin shadow.

Apparently noticing her friend's preoccupation, Miranda glanced around, waved at Kevin, then swung back to Sam. "Well, those two were the last pair I expected to see here."

"You and me both," Sam agreed. "Anyway, as I was saying, it's like we're in a town of left-brains and right-brains."

Tables had filled up quickly, and now Lucy was seating the dynamic duo at a table separated by only a few feet.

"Make that *half*-brains," retorted Jack's deep voice.

Sam twisted her neck around, then scowled. "This is a *private* luncheon, Jack. Or had you failed to notice?"

"I *didn't* fail to notice that we *didn't* get the table we asked for. We do have a meeting with an important client." Jack's voice boomed after Lucy.

Sam rolled her eyes and hissed, "Oh, why do I bother? Once a boor, always a boor."

"Or a wild boar," Miranda mumbled.

"Beware the tusks," Sam said, spearing a morsel of her seafood.

Lucy, having returned, asked, "Sorry, Mr. Sawyer? Did you want to be reseated?"

"We most certainly do. As far from *this* corner as possible."

"How about the *opposite* corner at the far end of the restaurant?"

"Fine. And when my client Mr. Clarke arrives, direct him there."

"Of course." Lucy led the two men away.

"Well, that's a relief," said Sam. "Okay, kiddo. Your turn. What's going on with you?"

Miranda paused, then answered her question with a question of her own. "What do you do when you have a weird dream?"

"Write it down," Sam answered without hesitation.

Miranda smiled. "You and your journals. How long have you been writing them?"

Sam looked out at the water as though it would help her see through time. "I really can't remember *not* journaling."

"I can't imagine writing so much," Miranda reflected. "I do keep journals, but they're mostly sketches and paintings. I'm thinking about turning my miniature watercolors into postcards I can send out to people. But writing down my thoughts on a regular basis just for myself? Not likely."

"Well, you record your thoughts in a different way, with your art," Sam observed.

"I figured I was just recording what's *out there*, not really recording my own impressions. Never saw it that way, but I suppose you're right."

The two friends spent the rest of their lunch sharing other news, their mutual surprise that summer was nearly over, and discussing some of the details of their current projects.

"Hate to say it," Sam remarked, "but I really have to get back to work." She placed cash inside the bill wallet the waitress had brought while they were talking.

"So do I." Miranda added her money to Sam's. "The docent here at the nursery lent me a pamphlet and I want to review it."

Sam smiled. "That's one of the things I love about your work, Miranda, that you pay such attention to the details."

Chapter 5

Miranda felt the hairs on the back of her neck prickle, but she resisted turning to see who might be observing her.

If it were Lucy, she'd have said something. I prefer people to ask if they can watch. How would they like it if someone were sneaking around behind them, studying them while they tried to focus?

As an artist, she enjoyed working in the privacy of her studio, or out in the field, where she could enter a meditative state she thought of as "flow." But she had also participated in her first *plein air* painting foray with a local group of artists last spring, which had made her understand better natural curiosity that drew non-artists to watching a creative person at work. Still, the last thing she wanted to do here was draw a crowd that might disrupt the restaurant.

Well, not really drawing *a crowd,* drawing *a crowd.*

The play on words did little to ease her annoyance. If only she *could* work with words instead of paints. Would strangers walk over to someone who'd chosen a private, secluded spot to write, then demand the author read the manuscript aloud?

She glanced up to check the details of what she was adding to her painting—the shadow cast by a market umbrella at the far end of the garden. From behind her, she overheard an exchange between a husband and wife.

The woman's voice said, "Oh, she won't mind. Painters *like* to be noticed, you know. After all, they *want* folks to admire their work. Isn't that why they do it?"

"I suppose so, dear," the man answered.

Miranda heard the reluctance in his voice, and wished she could tell him his instincts were right.

Of course, Zelda McIntyre, her artist's rep, with her focus on sales and marketing, wouldn't agree at all. *Zelda would tell me to make the most of the opportunity. Thank them for their attention, and send them to the local gallery to buy my work. 'Course I value the sales. But I have to listen to my heart, trust my own process.*

A lecture began to build in Miranda's brain—logical and articulate—on the vital need to synchronize head and heart. It developed into a detailed explication of her own need, as a wildlife painter, to retune her senses to the natural world, breathe with the landscape, quiet the human chatter to be able to hear the animal conversations already in progress.

She'd come to love the process above all else. The listening—first to silence, then to the million small sounds that emerged under it; the looking at the surface colors, then waiting till the actual hues revealed themselves and the deeper seeing would begin.

While the layperson's eye skipped over objects in an efficient and rapid series of identifications, the artist allowed things to resolve back into their component parts, where their individual elements could be seen, then chosen, then shared.

From Miranda's perspective, humans didn't live alone but in a rich sea of life to be cherished and understood, to teach grand lessons and inspire higher thoughts. She couldn't fail to notice the hush that fell over birds when a human shouted across a garden or blasted leaves aside with a blower whose motor obliterated all other sound within its radius.

Suddenly, a vibrant burst of color flashed into the corner of Miranda's eye. The couple who'd been talking behind her stepped into view right beside her art-table, the woman wearing lime polyester that shone unnaturally bright against the wooden tables and eucalyptus trees.

The man exclaimed, "Oh, look at those exquisite little paintings!"

"Well, if you *like* that sort of art." The woman now addressed Miranda. "Young lady? I think you can do better with that ocean color, don't you? It just isn't quite right."

The man blanched. "Ezmeralda!"

The woman's face took on an aspect of Mighty Purpose. "Well, some days it *is* that dark, but not in summer."

The husband's hands lifted briefly, then plunged into his pockets where they rattled change.

The woman leaned in for another look at the unfinished piece. "No," she confirmed, "never in summer."

Interesting that she noticed the darker shade. Should I bother to explain? An entire lesson in painting began to play through Miranda's mind: choosing the type of paint appropriate to the subject matter, using a practiced painter's eye that could observe the deepest hue in a multi-patterned surface like water, the concept of transparent color-layering, the technique of matching and applying that deeper color first.

Miranda and the woman's husband locked eyes for a moment. As though he'd received a full transmission of her thought, he grabbed his wife's hand and tugged at it.

"What?" the woman snapped.

"Hungry," he managed.

"Well, why didn't you just say so?" The woman rolled her eyes at Miranda. "These men and their stomachs!" She shook her head. "You keep painting, dear. Someday you might be real good." Jerking slightly as her husband yanked again at her hand, the Lime Woman smiled conspiratorially, then toddled across the garden.

Relieved the intrusion was over, Miranda inhaled deeply, dipped her brush in water to moisten it, then scrutinized her work-in-progress. The deeper colors seemed complete now: sapphires and green tourmalines, garnets and amethysts. *Time to study the lighter shades and mix new tones on my palette.*

A hummingbird sped past her like a bright piece of jewelry shot from a toy gun. Something about the sound seemed familiar. *Could that've been part of my dream?* She smiled, delighted to be keeping company with such a magical creature.

Then, as she swirled ochre into cerulean, she heard the shrieking woman's voice again. It wasn't laughing this time. It erupted into a scream, followed by the sad "ahhs" of other voices.

"Too bad," a man's voice resonated. "Hate it when a bird hits a window. This time it's a hummingbird, and it's dead."

Chapter 6

The hummer tried to see, but couldn't seem to open his eyes.

Open. Open.

He tried again, but his eyelids wouldn't respond.

Now he tried to move.

Move. Move.

He tried again, but his wings wouldn't respond either.

Dimly, he heard the deep rumble of human-sound, its incomprehensible waves and dips, like a dark ocean into which he'd fallen.

Must see. Must move. Babies in nest. North border protect. Food. Need food.

From high overhead he thought he could hear the familiar trill of his mate, but she sounded so very far away. Where is she? Where was he?

Here. Move.

If only he could get his wings to move, his eyes to open. He wanted to answer the high call of his mate, be about his daytime tasks with flowers and borders.

Light. Dark.

Everything had gone dark, though he knew it should still be day. Or had he somehow lost his way? Flown into a cave? No! Never. He knew his territory, stayed at his post dutifully. He knew, then, all was well, he'd done all things perfectly.

Trust. Know.

And now he floated. Not of his own power, but no longer adrift on that dark ocean of sound. Great Spirit had him.

Yield. Flow.

Chapter 7

Miranda heard the murmur of voices across the garden as it seemed to crescendo, a combination of concern and sadness.

A man's voice said "Pretty little thing. Too bad there's nothing we can do."

A younger man's voice countered, "Maybe we should call someone."

Miranda wondered if she should intervene on the bird's behalf. *Bet it's a hummer, and it's probably only stunned.*

Across the garden, she saw the group of people—Mr. and Mrs. Lime, plus another couple her own age—a well-built man standing beside an attractive woman with frosted hair.

Lime Woman spoke next. "Oh, just throw it away."

Miranda leapt from her bench. Hurrying over to the group gathered around the felled bird, she exclaimed, "No!"

Startled, the people turned to look at her.

"I'm . . . I'm sorry," she stammered. "It's just . . . leave it to me. Usually, they're just stunned. I'll take care of it."

Lime Woman's speaking voice cut the air like a buzz saw. "Well, I think I know when something's *dead*."

Paying no attention to that comment, Miranda knelt and studied the tiny creature. *So delicate!* Miranda held her breath and lifted him carefully—fearing even her gentle pinch between thumb and forefinger would crush him—then transferred him to her palm.

After giving the crowd her best reassuring smile, she walked with care back to her spot. Sitting at the bench by her art-table, she gazed at the creature in her hand. She utterly rejected the notion that the bird was dead, though no physical evidence supported her claim. *No movement; no heartbeat that I can detect; no respiration.* Yet, with an innate certainty, she knew. *He's alive.* His inert body lay in perfect stillness while she admired his exquisite details. "Thank you," she whispered. "I never thought I'd be allowed to get so close."

Indeed, she felt she'd been given a rare gift, and her painter's eye was going to take full advantage. "You're holding still just for me, aren't you?" she cooed. Though her diminutive model didn't reply, she considered this to be a conversation.

Entranced by his colors and the fine definition of his feathers, she examined the multi-layered tonalities that produced his tourmaline iridescence. "This is so kind of you," she said quietly. "What can I do to return the favor?"

He's granting me a fervent wish. What would his *be?* Glancing around the garden, she surmised this must be close to an ideal spot to have as his domain. But perhaps he'd wish for a few changes: annuals and perennials all in perpetual bloom; fewer humans, and surely he'd wish for no clear plates of glass.

She took a plain white hankie from her bag and placed the tiny bird on it, then secured him on her lap. Setting aside the nearly completed five-by-eight portrait of the garden she'd done earlier, she pulled out a fresh Claybord of the same size.

I know exactly what to do for you, my little friend. I bet you're dreaming now. I'll paint your dream.

The hummer floated.

Float. Flow. Listen.

He tried to get an aural fix. The ocean should be west, but he couldn't hear it. Couldn't hear wind through the trees, water burbling in the fountain. But a gentle, cooing sound was reaching him.

Strange sound. Nice sound.

But maybe, he worried, he couldn't hear the water because he was too close to it. That was it! He'd fallen into the fountain and was hearing everything from underwater!

Must fly!

With a tremendous surge of energy, he willed himself up and out of the water—out of the pond that sucked at him and tried to hold him under—aiming himself like a bullet for a blue sky.

Free! Air! Sky!

He soared, he plummeted, circled, spun, swooped, flipped, then hovered. But the aerodynamics seemed oddly different today: the air heavier—or himself lighter. Making one more circle, he tried to get his bearings.

Ocean? Gone. Mountain? Missing.

Panic raced through his heart. Hadn't he fallen into the fountain? And hadn't he raised himself through the water to reclaim his own piece of the air? But where was he? And where was his garden?

He looked down.

What he saw nearly made him fall from the sky again.

It was himself he saw! Asleep on a little white bed. Over him bent a human making sounds, holding a funny long stick in her hand.

Miranda swished her brush in water and spoke softly to the tiny patient in her lap. "Let's see how you like *this* garden."

I've painted the realistic garden, more or less. Now I need to create a dream-garden. I can use the same layout and perspective . . . that'll save time. The new version should have every flower the hummer'd love, no matter whether it'd really grow here or not.

She started working as fast as she could, color flowing from the end of her brush. Using lavender, she painted holly-hocks, some with petals closed, some open, like ballerinas in jets and pirouettes across a backdrop of green.

She'd studied the docent's pamphlet, never imagining she'd make such extensive use of it so quickly. But there seemed an urgency about this painting, as though her new little friend needed it and wouldn't be whole until all the details of his dream garden were captured on the Claybord.

Miranda lost track of time, absorbed in her task. Then she leaned back to review the piece. *It's almost complete now.* Just as a hummer would, she'd ignored scent and chosen flowers for their color and nectar. Spires of foxglove made a purple burst, and beyond it, she'd wanted something whim-sical, and had chosen a strawberry tree with its look-alike red blossoms. In the distance shone the bright blue where she'd painted in the ocean.

The lower right burst with the cheery pink of an azalea bush, and behind it lurked some partially obscured, pale blue irises. In her mind she'd been working to coax them out from their hiding place, but they resisted shyly. Their petals fluttering, stems aquiver, they stood together like bridesmaids waiting to march down the aisle.

Mid-level on the right side sprouted a bottlebrush bush with its self-descriptive red blooms; wide, flat hot-pink petunias seemed ready to offer their nectar. Balancing them on the left she'd placed a lilac bush with towering blossoms as elaborate as fancy ladies' hats.

The visionary garden had an arbor tucked into a corner, twined with honeysuckle, its flowers like handfuls of narrow white and pink satin ribbons tied intermittently to its vines. *This is one flower that'll please us both.* The hummingbird would love the sweet nectar, and Miranda could almost inhale their intoxicating perfume.

A few minutes later, her eye traveled across the wildly vivid array that now spread across her Claybord. Red-orange butterfly weed stood like bunches of crepe paper tied to tall, feathery stalks; ultra-orange nasturtiums poked their heads above dense leaves, and yellow hibiscus blossoms looked ready to spin, busy as little propellers in the breeze.

As the centerpiece of the garden grew a fuchsia, its drooping pink blossoms resembling acrobat dancers who hung from ropes, skirts flying up, blouses plumped with air, long arms reaching down.

Now I need to put the hummer in his garden, right in the center. He'll love the fuchsia. Hovering close, his beak ready to plunge, the small bejeweled bird began to appear brushstroke by brushstroke.

Chapter 8

The hummer tried to understand.

Know. Think. Know.

Something stirred in his mind, urging him to make sense of things.

All is life. Life is good. I am life.

How could he be in two places at the same time? He couldn't be hovering somewhere above himself and still actually *be* himself and be where he belonged.

So that could only mean one of the two images of himself was a pretend-image.

He'd seen glimpses like this before. Darting near human-places, he'd see another hummer right in his own territory. But on closer inspection, the intruder would match his own movements exactly.

Mirage. Water was like that sometimes, offering a picture, bouncing it back.

The hummer looked down again, certain the false image would have disappeared by now.

He's still there! He must be real, then. *My garden! Must fight!*

He dove, expecting his adversary to engage, spin and twirl, buzz and sing. Instead, he twirled through the thin air by himself, downward past the high branches, till he found himself lying on the soft white cloth.

Eyes closed, his chest constricted, his head throbbing, his feathers heavy. Then that familiar, comforting sound reached him.

Reply. Must reply so the nice sound wouldn't stop.

Know. Think. Know.

He could feel his beak opening slightly.

More of the sound.

Blink. Blink. Blink.

Yes! Awake! But more. Everything was more! He remembered colors—but these were brighter, clearer.

With every ounce of strength he possessed, he spread his wings in ever-so-slight a gesture. The sound came again as if encouraging him.

Lift. Flap. Lift.

He felt his body lighten, saw the white cloth get smaller below him. His body was his own again—the air fresh, the sunlight warm. He wanted to trill and soar, swoop and dart.

But first, he must *know* the source of the sound. The human sat watching him as if light were coming out of her face, and still making the nice noises.

Kind. Soft. Strong.

Hovering close, he looked in her giant's eye and saw his own reflection. Then he turned and saw the garden framed in front of her.

Different. Not his daytime garden. All contained in a kind of window, this was the garden he saw every night when he dreamed.

All here. His favorite flowers, bushes, trees, his most resonating colors; his most cherished nectars, enough to let him sip his way to heaven.

How here? He wondered how he could see his night-garden here in the daylight, and then he understood. This human was a dream-maker. Only Spirit could have shown her this. She'd made him his very own map of his heart's desire.

How tell her? Though he wondered if her huge, slow eye could see his quick one, for a heartbeat he closed his in acknowledgment.

Miranda had been so sure it would happen, she couldn't feign surprise when it did.

One moment he was moving his tiny beak, as though trying to tell her some important secret. She hadn't let him stop at that, but had encouraged him to keep on.

Then he blinked. That startled little eye seemed to acquire such a knowing look, as though fresh inspiration infused his compact being.

How long they continued their intimate communion, she couldn't say, losing track of time in proportion as she gained his trust.

The actual instant of lift-off, she missed, her human eye no match for his fleet body. But what she *did* see was his pausing mid-air to look first at her, then at her painting. Though for her it had been a matter of seconds, she calculated that in hummingbird-time, he'd probably spent several minutes studying the dream garden as though acknowledging its every bloom.

Then he turned back to look at her again. She held her breath, in awe of his apparent recognition. *Did he wink at me? I could swear he did.* And then he was gone.

Her communion with the small creature in the garden had wiped Miranda's mind clean of her usual concerns. Almost in a trance, she capped her paint tubes and cleaned her brushes, closed her bag and folded her art-table.

Later she would assess the painting, checking it for balance and clarity, composition and tonality. But for today, it had served its purpose, and so had she. It was enough to feel the sense of grace settling around her heart.

"Thank you," she murmured, making her way toward the exit. "Thank you for sharing your dream."

Suddenly, the hummer whirred past Miranda's head, louder than a bumble bee and close enough to touch. Then he sped to the far end of the garden and evanesced beyond her line of sight.

"No," he seemed to say. "Thank *you*."

Chapter 9

Miranda carried a steaming mug of tea from her kitchen put to her deck, this week's edition of the *Milford-Haven News* under her arm.

Settling into her hammock, she opened the paper, interested to see that below the fold a bold headline read, *CHARM OF A HUMMINGBIRD.*

Miranda chuckled and took a sip of tea, looking forward to reading about the little birds she loved. The local reporter Emily Wilkins always seemed to have her finger on the pulse of the town.

Monday, August 21, 1996
Milford-Haven, California
Visitors described an unusual event that took place at the Rosencrantz & Guildenstern Café. According to several witnesses, a dead bird was brought back to life.

Miranda put down her tea and swung her legs over the side of the hammock, paying closer attention to the article. *This sure sounds familiar. I totally forgot I talked with Emily about the hummer.*

Groups of the small birds are referred to as a "charm of hummingbirds." Two species reside on the Central Coast: the Anna's hummingbirds stay year-round; the Rufous are a migrating species who spend the warmer months here. Which species was involved in the incident was unclear to observers, as both have red feathers on or near their heads.

"The hummer flew right into an exterior wall of glass," Mr. Jack Sawyer reported. "I saw that much. After that I lost interest and walked away."

"I saw the hummer hit too," Mr. Kevin Ransom confirmed. "And the people nearby said it was a shame, and wanted to toss in the trash. But then Miranda, she said no, and went over to pick it up. I had to leave with my boss then, but I was hoping she'd help the little critter." Ransom is employed by Jack Sawyer of Sawyer Construction.

Oh my word, I didn't know they'd seen it happen. Then, as she continued reading, she groaned at the quotation from a Mrs. Ezmeralda Worthington, realizing this could only be the woman she'd nicknamed "Mrs. Lime."

"I told that young woman it was the height of foolishness to think she could raise a pitiful creature from the dead. But she just couldn't let it rest in peace. She actually picked it up and carried it off, and then appeared to be talking to it. I mean, what kind of people live in this town, anyway?"

Artist Miranda Jones, a local resident, had been invited to paint in the café garden that day. Her easel was set up in the far corner, away from diners, but close enough to hear the commotion following the bird's fatal flight.

When asked about the incident, the artist explained, "Hummingbirds draw their strength from the sugar found in many flowers. But having lost consciousness, the hummer couldn't drink. I felt his presence, though, and thought I might be able to reach him telepathically."

Miranda felt suddenly embarrassed, as though she were some woo-woo weirdo who fancied she could talk with animals. *And that's exactly what Mrs. Lime thinks of me. Now everyone who reads the paper will think so too.*

And yet, she *had* communicated with the tiny bird somehow. Her only explanation was that by focusing on his favorite flowers in her own mind, she had projected images that encouraged or reassured him to come back from whatever dream he'd been temporarily locked into.

She took a breath, and continued reading.

Whatever her method, Ms. Jones was able to help the bird, who regained consciousness and resumed his flight through the garden. "Musta been body warmth," one diner declared. Another said, "That bird wasn't dead, just dazed."

"Could be an example of interspecies communication," remarked a visiting physicist.

Would the hummer have come back to life without the assistance of one concerned citizen? Those who viewed the incident can only speculate.

Ultimately, it may be the artist who had the last word. "Cetaceans communicate in part by transmitting pictures," Ms. Jones said. "Perhaps avian species do as well. We still have so much to learn about the animals with whom we share the planet. I certainly learned from the hummingbird that he was as aware of me as I was of him. That's a start."

Chapter 1

Veronica Jones lifted the monogrammed napkin from her lap and touched it to the corners of her mouth. Folding the smooth cloth in half, she pulled it through the silver napkin ring that bore the same initials as the linen.

The sun room where she and her husband—and their daughters, when they were home—usually shared breakfast felt chilly but cheerful with early forsythia blooms in the garden emanating vivid yellow through French doors and tall windows.

Veri, as her family and friends called her, looked across the small table at her husband of many years—still handsome and straight-backed, the gray at his temples lending a distinguished touch to his sculpted face.

"I've got to do something about the girls," she said, eyeing the coffee pot and considering whether she'd allow herself another half cup.

"You're always doing something about the girls," Charles said, not even looking over the top of the *San Francisco Chronicle* he read religiously every morning.

"You know what I mean, Charles. One is living in that icy tower of glass; the other is practically buried in that basement. Neither of them is truly happy. Neither is really safe."

Charles folded his paper and looked into her eyes. "Don't fret, dear. They're grown women, now. You can't live their lives for them. You can't tell them what to do."

From his mollifying tone, and from the softness of his expression, she knew he sympathized. Still, his words rankled. She couldn't bear the idea of not being able to help her daughters —whether or not they asked. She had, in fact, come up with a plan. Well, a partial plan. Though she had no intention of revealing details to their father just yet, she did think a mention might be politic.

"Uh-oh," he said, shaking his head while he poured himself a fresh cup of coffee. "You're up to something. Let's have it."

"Well," she began, "it would save them both money, and they'd be far more secure."

Veri smiled, and when her husband squinted, she saw with satisfaction that amusement was already beginning to coax a smile at the edges of his mouth.

Good. I'll make him my co-conspirator before he even knows what he's sanctioning.

Meredith Jones pressed the button for 22 and closed her eyes as a gust of wind swirled through the lobby and sent a blast into the elevator. April breezes howled through the shaft until the doors fully closed, and she felt her heart lurch right along with the car as it climbed through the lower floors.

With a "ding," the doors flew open and she stepped onto the faux-marble floor, then clacked down the hallway to her unit, wrinkling her nose at the cooking smells that clung to the wallpaper in the corridor. Sliding the key into her lock, she pushed open her door and flung off her high heels even before the metal front door slammed shut behind her.

"Ahh," she said aloud, dropping her briefcase, throwing her coat over the back of a bar stool, and opening the fridge. She reached inside for a half-finished bottle of Chardonnay, poured herself a glass, then settled on the sofa, wiggling her toes as she stretched her legs across the cushions.

Missed it again, she said, bemoaning that she never managed to get home in time to see the sunset. *But what little I saw from the car was gorgeous.*

For a new VP of client relations at a high-powered financial management firm, working late came with the territory. Still, she felt entitled to complain in the privacy of her own apartment. When her stomach rumbled, she remembered that bellyaching wouldn't put food on her table.

"Pizza Palace?" she wondered aloud. They did have a great Italian salad. Sezchuan Sensations sounded more appealing, though, and she stepped to the kitchen counter, picked up the handset with her favorite restaurants programmed into the speed-dial function, and placed the call.

By the time she'd changed into her dove-gray sweat pants and zippered top, prepared a tray, and turned on her TV, the intercom began buzzing.

A few minutes later, while she deftly picked at her Szechuan chicken and spicy string beans, she rewound the tape in her VCR and hit play, laughing out loud when Kramer, looking as if he'd just stuck his finger in an electrical outlet, walked across the hall and into Jerry's apartment to ask an inane question. It was a show about . . . nothing, Meredith decided, which was why she enjoyed watching it. How else could she take her mind off the daily stress and unwind?

Suddenly the crisp bite of spicy chicken trapped between her chop sticks didn't look as delicious as it had a moment earlier. *I've managed to avoid thinking about it for a whole hour and half, and now it's back, dammit.*

Albert Rothman, recently named senior partner—and the youngest ever to be so named—knew how brilliant he was, how valuable to the firm, and he had his eye on wealth to rival sultans. But he had a blind spot about his sex appeal. Convinced any woman would be grateful to be blessed by his attentions, he'd so far managed only to offend "lesser" employees, each of whom had been quietly dismissed with an attractive financial bonus. And Meredith only knew about these arrangements because she herself had now made partner.

Today, however, he'd managed to offend her twice, in two distinct ways. First, he'd questioned her data interpretation at her debut partner presentation. Though it'd stung, she'd accepted the criticism graciously, acknowledging the new alpha dog, flattering him by treating him as leader, though in truth he was only a couple of years older than she.

Second, he'd propositioned her. *Talk about a no-win scenario*, Meredith thought bitterly. She knew perfectly well how the game was played: be charming, but not overtly flirtatious; dress in a way that was appealing but not sexy; do your work better than any of the male partners.

A mentor had once said to her, "Meredith, in this business you have to be either very good, or very bad." She hadn't understood what he meant at first, so he'd explained. "If you plan to sleep your way to the top, be strategic and don't get emotionally involved. If you *don't* plan to use sex to get ahead, be sure not to sleep with *anyone* to get ahead. It'll be used against you."

Best advice I ever got, she mused. She'd adhered to his suggestion, and never dated anyone at the firm. In fact, she felt professional behavior at work was the gold standard. She also felt that what she did on her own time was her own business.

She glanced at her chopsticks as though she had no idea what to do with them and set them aside as her thoughts came back to Albert. Their paths were entwined at work. Would she be interested in dating him if not? Her instincts told her he was too self-involved and though too little of women to truly hold her interest. In any case, because of their work connection, the point was moot. Her own personal rules wouldn't allow involvement with him.

So where did that leave her now? *Damned if I do, damned if I don't.* If she turned him down, he'd take offence, and try his best to take it out of her career performance, one way or another. If she accepted his invitation—drink and dinner for now, but who knows what he really expected—she'd be stepping into a quagmire.

"Hell with it," she said, pressing the fast forward button on her remote. "I'm *not* going out with that man."

She took a deep breath and looked out the picture window at the view of the city now sparkling against a field of black. Between adjacent tall buildings, she could see the string of lights outlining the Golden Gate Bridge.

If she lost her job, she'd certainly have to move out of this apartment with its privileged views. But that wouldn't be the end of the world.

With the mental toughness that'd ensured her rapid ascent in a male-dominated career, she refused to think about Albert any longer. Instead, she swept away the debris of her dinner, took a hot bath, set her alarm, and curled up with a steamy romance novel. In her fantasies, a real relationship with a good man was well within the realm of possibility.

Miranda Jones pushed more Cadmium Yellow Medium Hue paint from the tube onto her pallette. To it, she added a touch of Hansa Yellow, then experimented by using her brush to swipe through a touch of Naples, just to see whether the mixture would give her the variation of depth she wanted.

She loved the Daniel Smith paint: the luminous, vivid transparency, how easy they were to work with, and how permanent the hues. She also liked that she could get the same array of colors, whether she worked in watercolor, or in oils, as she did today.

She glanced around the Bays Arts Co-op Studio and Gallery where she was one of several artists who rented space. More than a cubicle, less than a closed room, each of them had three standing walls on which to hang completed pieces, plus work tables, easels, small display tables, and bins for posters and prints.

Two slots away from the large plate glass window in front, Miranda's heard some comings and goings, but paid no attention, lost in her work.

This April, she found herself craving the color yellow. Every touch of it drew her eye, whether of a forsythia bush in bloom, a school bus trundling by, or a bright canary umbrella on someone's balcony.

By training and by inclination, she usually painted from life: from seeing something, seeing *into* it, or studying its surface, or sometimes even seeing *through* it to notice the layer behind, and how that context affected her understanding of the subject. Sunset on clouds, distant hills, tiny grasses less than a foot away, the eyelashes on a big cat, the muscled stance of a buck silhouetted on a ridge. All of it mattered, informed her consciousness, and spoke to her heart.

There were others days that she painted from an inner vi-sion—a close-up detail she hadn't realized she'd noticed, or an "inscape" that began to take form. Today was one of those days. She'd become aware of this morning, as though puzzle pieces began to assemble. By this afternoon, she knew she'd have no choice but to access the developing image by the most direct route—picking up her paint brush. It'd felt electric today, when brain-met-hand-met-brush-met-paint-met-paintboard.

And most of it was coming out yellow. *Well, I suppose spring itself is pouring through me out onto the paper.* Then, suddenly, it seemed complete. The upper portion of the image was bright, solid blue; the middle, a band of sapphire; the front, a high wall of hundreds of tiny blossoms in bloom, each its own shade of yellow, and all of them iterations of mustard.

It's gotta be in bloom all over the hills south of here. I just have to go see them for myself.

Prologue

Broadcast journalist Christine Christian stepped down from her black car into an even blacker night.

She extended her leg past the running board of the Ford Explorer, waiting till her shoe found the hardened dirt of the rutted road. *Actually, I'm inside the gates, so this'll be the driveway,* she thought, barely able to see the ground since dousing her headlights.

Cool sea wind tumbled through the air, carrying with it the fresh tang of kelp. Her hair ruffling, she glanced overhead to look for the moon. *I know it's nearly full, and it rose early tonight.* But the sky appeared moonless, and such stars as normally sparkled in the clear, windswept autumn air were obscured by dense cloud cover.

A hundred feet below the bluff, the sea pounded. An October storm had been traveling the South Pacific, and even this far north, the Central Coast reverberated with the effects. "Generating winds of up to fifty miles per hour . . . " she remembered her KOST-SATV colleague saying on this evening's broadcast.

On her left, the terrain fell away to the ocean—now nothing more than an inky, undulating mass. To the northwest, the flash of the Piedras Blancas lighthouse winked in the darkness, sweeping across the landscape to reveal a ghostly skeleton of the unfinished mansion.

Even by its outline, she could tell this Clarke House held something special in its design. Having studied the architectural drawings, she found the reality of the physical structure intriguing. Though she'd read that some of the locals objected to its massive size being ostentatious and out of place, she could see it also fit the site as though it belonged. *The way skyscrapers fit Manhattan.*

The image of a cityscape seemed incongruous, and she stood still a moment longer, waiting for it to make sense. *Funny, when I was a kid growing up in this little town, all I wanted to do was get away—get to a big city. And I did. But now I find myself drawn back here.* Yes, that was it . . . processing the fact that, after her many travels, she should find herself once again in Milford-Haven.

For one thing, there was the job with KOST in Santa Maria. After several years on-camera for the broadcast networks—mostly NBC —she'd made the switch to satellite. Just this month the FCC's deregulation of the market had become official, and 1996 would probably make the history books as a turning point for the TV business. She'd taken the title of Special Correspondent, which meant decent pay and great freedom to develop her own content. Her three-part piece on adoption had just been shown in the Central Coast region. *Part three aired Sunday—two days ago.*

She was already gathering material for her next three-parter on earthquakes, a story that would be taking her to San Francisco, then to Japan and to Turkey. *My bags are all packed.*

I'm spending three days in San Fran researching the '89 Loma Prieta quake. Then I leave for Tokyo from there.

Now, there was *this* story that had brought her to Milford-Haven. *What a strange homecoming. I should come back in the daylight, visit the newspaper where I had my first job . . . see what's the best little spot for breakfast these days . . . walk on Touchstone Beach. If my wandering soul has a home, it's probably here.*

Chris took a step away from the bluff, aware once again of the dark that surrounded her. *What am I doing here now? Pursuing a lead, as usual.* She sighed. *Better get this over with. Wish I'd worn sturdier shoes than these flats.* Chilled in the wind, she pulled her jacket closer and drew on the pair of leather gloves she'd tucked in her pocket.

Adjusting the long diagonal strap of the compact purse she wore slung across her body, she hefted her flashlight and clicked it on. She picked her way over construction debris and uneven terrain toward the front of the house, where eventually stairs would lead up to the entrance. Stepping onto a narrow plank that trembled under her feet, she dashed upward, then leapt off to stand just inside the foyer. *Ack! I thought it was dark outside—but inside it's pitch black.*

Chris stood still, trying to focus. Minutes passed, yet her pulse wouldn't settle. Shifting her feet, she tried to find a piece of floor unlittered with . . . what? Nails, concrete clumps, snips of wire? Still she waited, hoping her eyes would make a further adjustment to the unrelieved darkness.

The house seemed to sway with the wind and crashing surf, unsteady on its underpinnings. *That's an illusion, I'm sure. It's my own legs that're unsteady. Dammit it, Chris! You know what they say about Curiosity.*

She stood in what would undoubtedly be the living room —an expanse framed by a crosswork of beams, exposed for now, with a space left open on one whole side for a future wall of glass. *I was right. The lines are good, and the view will be spectacular.*

On the opposite wall, flagstone had already been fashioned into an oversized fireplace. It seemed curiously complete in this incomplete room—except for the rectangular hole with the ends of a ladder just visible.

The plans showed a hearthstone goes there—imported marble. She'd noticed this detail had shown up on both sets of plans. *Remember, one detail can make the story.* Reed had always told her that, and he was the best reporter in the business. *He did get in trouble once, though, covering that story in Ohio. Safe home after reporting in Vietnam, and then he's almost killed in that deserted house. He told me later he had the feeling he shouldn't go there.*

A chill swept over her now, and the fine hairs on the back of her neck tingled. *What's my intuition saying? I should leave this place.* This swaying, unhallowed structure menaced with its protruding metal splinters and ragged concrete edges.

But what was this so-called intuition that she shouldn't have come here? Wasn't that just fear? After all, she'd been led to this location—vectored here by one clue after another. *I can either be a wimp, or a good reporter. Logic says there's something to be discovered. I have to find out what.*

The first clue had been little more than an inkling . . . *or more like a rankling,* she recalled. Learning a mansion was being built in Milford-Haven—a first for the cozy artist-town —she'd called Sawyer Construction for an interview. Foremost among her list of questions was whether or not the likelihood of a new earthquake code would present fresh challenges either to design or to construction.

Geography, geology, seismology . . . these were three of Chris's pet subjects. Ever since the 1994 Northridge earthquake, she'd been tracking not only press coverage, but also published scientific papers about the possibility of new building codes. That quake had included what the seismologists called "unexpected moment frame damages." FEMA was now looking carefully at steel strength and possible detrimental effects on connection design.

Before conducting any interview, Chris always did careful research to be better prepared with good questions. *But,* she admitted, *I also do it to butter-up my subject.* The odd thing was that Jack Sawyer—rather than being flattered by the attention of a reporter who could speak at least some of his own language—had seemed by turns diffident and defensive and, ultimately, disingenuous. *A man with something to hide?*

A sound—a snap of fabric?—yanked her from her thoughts and sent her heartrate skyrocketing. She held her breath and heard the sound again. Like an exhalation, plastic wrapped over vacant window openings was sucked and pulled against the tape holding it to the framework. *Just the wind.* Perhaps the house itself was breathing, trying to expel its bad humors.

Chris took a step onto something that rolled under her foot, throwing her off balance. She caught herself by bracing against a low cinderblock wall, tearing a piece of skin from her palm. She yelped in the dark, but at least the jab of pain had served to sharpen her attention.

The reasons she'd come here began to return to her mind in an orderly progression. First, there'd been the call from an anonymous tipster that there might be something strange about the plans for the Clarke House. She'd confirmed this with her own investigation, discovering the house had *two sets* of plans. She'd needed an explanation, but hadn't wanted to tip her hand to Sawyer too soon.

Then my source called me again. He was right about the plans. Chances are he's right in everything he says about this house. He was an illusive informant—a phone contact she thought of as "Mr. Man," since he refused to give his namewho called with tantalizing fragments of information. She tried to fit them together like so many shards of broken crystal, clear and sharp-edged.

He'd said to meet him here, so here she was trying to gather more fragments of this story, and she found herself resenting it. *Joseph will be waiting at Calma with a clandestine dinner for two. Tonight's our make-up date after our little tiff. He planned a midnight supper . . . all the more romantic for the secrecy, the hour . . . and the rapprochement.*

The thought hastened her, and she tried again to focus on the incomplete room. Lifting her flashlight, she began inspecting the spaces framed by raw beams. She stepped through an opening. *This will be the kitchen.* She could see where the crew had marked identifiable icons for drains and faucets, lines to indicate cabinets and pantry. *All of this seems normal enough. Where's the story? I wonder what Mr. Man wants to show me?*

One thing that'd varied between the two sets of plans was something about the steel: different manufacturers, but also different grades. She figured a quick look at exposed steel beams under the house would reveal which steel had actually been used.

How do I get down there? She walked from the kitchen across the expanse of the living room and discovered a stair-well against the far wall. But at the moment it contained neither stairs nor a plank. She thought back for a moment. *Oh . . . there was a ladder in that opening by the fireplace.* Cursing again, she began walking carefully toward the gaping hole.

Just then another sound reached her—closer than the persistent wind and crashing surf. *What was that? A scrape . . . footfall? Or is that Mr. Man? About time he got here. But I didn't see any headlights. What if it's not him?* Clicking off her flashlight, she pressed her body against the closest beam. *I'm alone in a windswept rattletrap of wood beams and metal scraps, and I should've been home doing my nails before driving to Santa Barbara to meet Joseph.*

She breathed deeply and tried to picture herself arriving home, refreshing her polish and makeup, locking the door behind her, starting the SUV's engine. *Details.* They were always her best defense against fear.

She listened a moment longer, hearing no further scraping. *Just my nerves.* She clicked her flashlight back on, then continued toward the hearth-well. The ladder itself seemed to disappear into the depths. "It's the blackest hole I've ever seen," she muttered. "Blacker than a black cat's ass—on black velvet."

"There's a quick way down there, Ms. Christian."

"Ahh!" She whirled toward the voice that'd burst out of nowhere. "Who—?" *That's not my contact's voice.* Her throat spasmed, and she gulped air, her heart pounding louder than the surf. "Where—?" She gasped. "You just about scared the. . . ." Struggling for calm, she clutched her flashlight and tried to keep its beam from bouncing across the man's features.

His seamed face loomed over a hulking physique. *Any distinguishing marks? Yes! I thought it was a shadow, but that's a mole on his left cheek . . . size of a quarter. Can't really see his eyes.* She inhaled. "What . . . what are you doing here?"

"The question should be what are *you* doing here, Ms. Christian. *I* work here." The voice was steady, self-assured.

"Of course you do." *Why does he know my name?* She struggled for a casual tone. "Good thing you're here, because I could really use some help." A laugh erupted from her throat like a burst of static from a malfunctioning radio. "Actually, I wanted to look around in the basement, but it's so hard to see in the dark."

The guy said nothing. Chris wondered how long she could keep producing an uninterrupted stream of words, hoping to use them like a protective force field. *Keep talking. Redirect the focus to him.* "Say, you didn't even bring a flashlight."

"Very observant."

Get a conversation going. "Guess we both counted on moonlight."

"Not with these clouds."

"You must know the house real well if you work here." *Burly muscles, heavy work boots.* "One of the construction crew, huh?"

"Right again."

"Well, listen, I'm running late for an appointment and someone's waiting for me. He tends to get upset when I'm not on time. I'll come back in the daylight when I can see better." She made a move away from the hearth-well, but it only brought her closer to him. As she took another step, her foot caught on something, pitching her forward.

The worker's arm shot out in front of her, his large hand capturing hers as she regained her balance. *He couldn't stop the impulse to catch me.* She stood toe-to-toe with him now, and could smell alcohol on his breath as he exhaled. *Probably a bourbon drinker*, she noted, unable to stop cataloguing details.

His hand opened suddenly. She slipped hers free and stepped back. *Has his brief moment of gallantry put him enough off balance that I can appeal to him? Don't I always reach people with my authenticity and with my words?* She looked up into the weathered face, trying to make eye contact, but could see nothing more than a glint. "Thanks so much for taking care of me."

He paused, then smiled. "Oh, I haven't taken care of you yet."

Damn! "But you're about to, am I right?"

A chuckle rumbled in his barrel chest. "Too right."

Good! Maybe I did reach him this time . . . I made him laugh. How many times have I talked my way out of a tight spot? How many times have I played out this kind of scenario in my head?

Time seemed to slow, and her perspective shifted until she watched the stand-off between herself and burly-guy from a slight distance, as though she were discussing the angle with her television camera crew. *It's an over-the-shoulder two-shot, like one of my interviews. Then we cut to a close-up that shows the mole, the craggy face—trying to give the audience a chance to read his expression.*

Now her view altered and the setting was a Western: a black-hatted hulk blocked the path of a red-dressed spit-fire. *Whose story is this? When did it happen? Why are we in the Old West?* She almost seemed to recognize the scene . . . from a story by her favorite writer, Louis L'Amour. *Never let the opponent gain the advantage,* his narration advised. *Don't wait. Make the first move.*

The scene shifted again, and now she saw herself as Emma Peel in *The Avengers*. Skilled in martial arts, undaunted by her precarious predicament, the heroine faces her adversary. *Emma kicks out with those long legs, takes her man by surprise.*

Suddenly, Chris found herself standing in her own shoes, opposite her own bad guy. He might be bigger, stronger, more massive, but maneuverability was on *her* side. *It's now or never!*

She clicked off her flashlight and hurled it at his head. She'd already chosen exactly what direction she would run— past him, not away, because that would be unexpected. In the sudden blackness she knew she'd have a second's worth of advantage. It was just the second she needed.

She leapt forward, and saw his fist too late. It impacted her temple with the force of an explosion, hurtling her backward into the gaping hearth-well. Her body seemed to hang for a moment, suspended in space—until it smashed against the dirt, forcing the last molecule of air from her lungs. *I can't breathe. I can't move.*

Her eyes blinked in the dark, her mind searched for options. She saw his huge feet land on the dirt near her, and kept her eyes still. *If he thinks I'm already dead he'll just leave me. Don't breathe!*

He was carrying something . . . a shovel. *No!* He stepped on its edge, forcing it into the big pile of soft earth, lifting a load of it, moving it toward her head.

Just before the dirt hit her face, she closed her eyes. *I'm covered enough now that he can't see me. I'll breathe soon.*

Another shovelful landed on her chest, its weight sodden. Now another was flung over her face.

It'd been too many seconds since air had found its way into her lungs, and with a sudden clarity, she realized she had never taken that breath.

Desperately, she inhaled, but she found no oxygen. Only the wet, sandy home-soil of the Central Coast.

Chapter 1

The autumn storm tore at the clouds covering Milford-Haven, revealing a swollen moon that hung over a coastline frothy with agitated surf.

Miranda Jones watched the distant flash of the lighthouse for a moment, then looked away from her window to focus on a narrow band of thick paper scrolled across her studio floor. Inhaling deeply, she dipped the tapered fibers of her immense paintbrush and struggled to lift its wet mass from the inky bucket, then swept a black streak across the white paper.

She held the three-inch diameter brush handle upright—its top reaching to her waist—and resumed her bent-knee, wide-footed stance. Hoisting the fully saturated brush, she began the dance that would drag it rhythmically along the paper, creating a vertical image.

Placing her bare feet on the sheet, she stepped backwards, the weight of the sodden brush causing her arms to shake. Yet each motion synchronized with both the soft *shakuhachi* flute music that played over her stereo, and with the call the paper itself seemed to be whispering in her ear.

When she reached the end of the sheet, she walked back to her starting point, replaced the brush in its bucket, and stood entranced, her soul soaking up the experience even as the image soaked into the paper.

By now her studio was permeated with the distinct aroma of the *sumi* ink. Concocted of palm ash and glue, it also contained traces of camphor and musk oil. She inhaled again, agreeing with the legend that promised the ink's special odor helped to induce the perfect meditative state.

She'd placed four black stones—smoothed and rounded from tumbling for years through the nearby surf—as weights to hold the scroll in place. Now they almost blended into the image, as though she'd added four extra smudges of ink. But, in fact, the stones would be removed and weren't part of what she'd painted. She scrutinized the piece. *When the stones are removed, will the piece look incomplete? Yes . . . it needs something more.*

She *felt* the idea, more than she *thought* it. Focusing on an unfilled portion of the paper, she reached for a smaller brush that stood ready in its own bucket. She lifted it, then let her hand sweep through a series of motions. When she'd replaced the smaller brush, she closed her eyes and bowed over the paper, signaling the completion of the current scroll. *My teacher would add a touch of vermillion . . . but I'm not ready for that yet.*

During art school a few years earlier, she'd completed a course on *sumi-e,* and since then she'd occasionally used the ancient Japanese ink-wash painting as both a meditation and a discipline. Traditionally, it was both, from the almost ritualistic grinding of the ink stone into water, to the careful handling of brushes whose hairs were trimmed to a delicate point.

But more recently she'd been accepted into a workshop by the eminent American calligrapher Barbara Bash, who'd shared her unique approach of pouring *sumi* ink from half-gallon bottles and using an oversized brush to create her huge scrolls. *I'll never master this the way Barbara has, but I love how it centers my mind. It's all about flow.*

Is this a "head" or a "heart" process? If "head" was the answer, it wouldn't be in an intellectual sense, because the ink almost seemed to be "thought-projected" onto the paper, the marks capturing a flow of movement uninterrupted by editorializing.

Though the actual painting of the ink-wash was necessarily quick, preparing for each piece was a lengthier process. *At least it is for a relatively inexperienced calligrapher like me.* The ink had to be poured, the paper laid, and the artist had to summon both energy and vision.

Miranda appreciated that this big-brush technique worked on three levels. As physical exercise, it felt similar to Tai Chi and to Yoga, both of which she enjoyed. As mental discipline, its immediacy permitted no distraction, no procrastination. A brush pressed a moment too long would cause ink to soak through and ruin both the paper and the image. She carried these lessons into her own watercolor work.

And though technically big-brush *sumi-e* was certainly a form of fine art, it was far enough away from her core practices of watercolor and acrylics, that it left her free from internal judgment. She could float above the brush, the paper and the image, allowing thoughts and feelings to surface freely. *I know why I love it so much. It lets my heart speak.*

The CD she was listening to came to an end, and a gust of wind rattled the windows. *How many images have I done tonight? The new one makes four. And how long have I been at this? I've lost track of time again.* She glanced out at the moon, noting it was lower now, its color beginning to shift from silver to gold as it sank toward the ocean. *It'll set soon, and we'll have some black sky before dawn, so I'll have a chance to sleep a little. I think I'm finished work for tonight.*

Stepping to her worktable, she picked up her X-acto knife and carefully sliced below the end of the painted image, separating it from the heavy roll. She lifted the top edge enough to drag the long sheet parallel to the others, which were laid out on the studio floor to dry. Tomorrow she'd mount the stepladder and tack the vertical images to the wall. For now, she stared down at the new work and its three companion pieces, finished earlier that evening.

She stood back to examine the four scrolls. "Oh!" she exclaimed. "It's the four seasons!" Amazed this hadn't occurred to her before, she now saw clearly that the four six-foot-high water paintings described the subtle elements of California's coastal seasons: a pine for winter; a blooming crape myrtle for spring; an olive tree for summer; and a persimmon tree for autumn. *Maybe I didn't notice at first because the images are black-and-white.*

The piece she'd just finished was of the persimmon, its signature drooping-leaves and multi-stemmed trunk so reminiscent of Asia. Yet she learned they'd been imported to California in the 1800s, and they were now as much a part of the Central Coast as any native tree. The bright orange color of the fruit came into her mind, highlighting the fall season when it ripened.

She glanced down at the bottom corner, where she'd added that final swirl of paint. *What is it? It looks like . . . a kitten!* Kneeling, she inspected the small image more carefully. *I know*

I had no particular definition in mind when I created it. She remembered laying the wet brush sideways, then dotting it here and there as she lifted it off the page. But now, there they were, the distinct feline features—head and whiskers, tail and feet.

"Hello," she said to the impish picture. "Thanks for the visit!"

Tired to the bone, Miranda stood, stretched and sighed. *Now for the cleanup.* It took her a good half hour to wash the brushes, empty the buckets, and secure anything else she might've left open in her workspace. By the time she flipped the light switch and headed downstairs to her bedroom, she was already half asleep.

I'll shower in the morning, she thought. *But it's already morning!* Too tired to make sense of the chronology, she washed her face, brushed her teeth and collapsed under her comforter. *It'd be nice to cuddle up with that little kitty I drew.* She smiled at the fantasy and imagined the kitty tiptoeing across the covers.

Those four scrolls . . . they're great, but I'd love to do them in full color. Maybe I can take the four seasons idea and incorporate it into my miniature watercolor postcards. . . .

As she reached to turn out the light on her nightstand, something caused her to choke. Gasping, she reached for the water bottle she kept handy by the bed, sputtering as she took a gulp. *What in the world?* It wasn't as though she'd gagged on a morsel of food, or swallowed down the wrong pipe. She'd been choking *before* she took the swig of water.

She shuddered, trying to sense the source of whatever she might be feeling. *Is something bad about to happen?*

No, not in Milford-Haven, she reassured herself. *Bad things don't happen here.*

Jack Sawyer's alarm clock stuttered into life, its plastic frame cracked from abuse. A heavy hand swept down and banged the "snooze" button, then retreated under the covers.

Jack hadn't slept well. Keeping one step ahead of town, county, and state regulations didn't usually keep him up at night. But now he had to contend with Samantha. No matter what he did, he could never seem to get away from that woman.

He swung his legs out from under the blanket and didn't notice its long-forgotten coffee stains. He focused for a moment on the clock's digital display. The last digit no longer illumnated, so it was always a guess. He hoped it was still within a minute or two of 7 a.m.

Jack headed down the hall, his bare feet leaving an occasional imprint in the dusty floor. An hour-and-a-half from now, he'd be in his office and the irritating phone calls would start: from contractors trying to pick his brains; from prospects who said other contractors could outbid him; from incompetent workers with idiotic questions; from inspectors with nasty notices. But at least his *home* phone wouldn't ring, and he wouldn't turn on his cell till later. Plus—today held the promise of a new client.

He reached the bathroom and scowled at himself in the mirror. The fierce blue eyes were still clear. The hair had gone salt-and-pepper, the face a little jowly. Chest and arms remained firm, thanks to the fact he spent about as much time on his job sites as behind his desk. Jack's gaze trailed down the rest of his six-foot frame—solidly packed with muscle, but with a little too much gut. *Not bad for over fifty. Besides, only one thing really matters. Everything still functions.*

Just then, his home phone did begin to ring. *Damn! Who the hell would be calling me now?* A sudden fit of coughing seized him, loud enough that he missed the next two rings of his phone, and on the fourth one his answering machine picked up.

"This is Jack Sawyer. I'm out. Leave a message if you expect me to call you back." He paid no attention to his own gravelly voice on the outgoing message. But after the beep, when an authoritative female voice began speaking, Jack started coughing again.

"Jack, this is Sam calling." As if he didn't know. *"I'll leave a message at your office, but in case you don't go there this morning, you should know you'll be facing an injunction. Have a nice day."*

Kevin Ransom loved the mornings better than any other time of day. In autumn, it was still dark and chilly when he got up. He never knew whether the sky would look pink or orange or lavender, so it was always a surprise. He liked that best of all.

The view from Kevin's porch raced down a steep incline through a stand of tall California pines. The smallness of the house was made up for by the size of the trees, which stood on protected land, so they'd never be cut down. The first rays of light penetrated the upper branches like the strobe lights of a *National Geographic* photographer. *Guess the storm last night cleared out all the clouds.*

The squirrel who occupied the back yard stepped onto the railing of the deck and walked gingerly toward Kevin, chattering for his morning nut. Today it would be a cashew, and Kevin couldn't decide whether his squirrel was demanding an early Halloween treat, or stocking up for winter.

Kevin only had a few minutes before he had to leave for work. He liked to get there before Mr. Sawyer and make sure the coffee was made. It sometimes seemed to make Mr. Sawyer's mood a little better.

"Hey, little fella." He spoke quietly so as not to scare the squirrel off. "Want another one?" he asked. He wondered why it was always so much easier to talk to animals than it was to talk to people.

Sally O'Mally unlocked the back door of her restaurant and flipped on the kitchen lights, illuminating the gleaming steel sinks, pristine countertops, and the rows of shiny pans that hung from a large overhead rack. She caught the room's faint odor of fresh lemons that lingered after last night's cleaning. Though she'd been tired when she woke up this morning, she felt a spark of energy at seeing her workspace spotless and ready for a new day.

Mama trained me well. Still, I never do get up as early as she does. She pictured her mother in Arkansas, still living on the farm, still knitting, and still baking up a storm—biscuits, breads, and her signature pies.

Gotta get the first pot o' coffee started. After putting her shoulder bag in the tiny private office she'd created out of a closet, she pulled the plastic lid off an industrial-sized tin of ground coffee, loaded several scoops into a filter paper, then snapped the basket-holder into place. *Okay, now for the biscuits. Maybe I can get the first batch in before June gets here.*

Her hands moved almost by their own volition as they found the chilled batter—prepared the night before—in the fridge, greased the baking sheets, dusted the cutting board, rolled out the dough and began pressing into it a round cutter. When the sheets were ready for the oven, she slid them in. Just then the back door swung open again.

"Morning, Sal," June called cheerily in her distinctive Brooklyn accent. "Geez, it's gettin' light a lot later already!"

"Well, that's September for ya," Sally confirmed. "How you doin' this mornin'?"

"Fine."

Sally smiled at the long sound of June's vowels. *I s'ppose I sound just as funny to her as she does to me. Milford-Haven brings in all kinds.*

Sawyer Construction Company was still closed and locked when early-morning sunlight slid past decade-old layers of dust on the Venetian blinds. There was no sign of life until the light on the office answering machine illuminated, and the cassette tape began to squeal softly while it turned.

Jack's outgoing message crackled over the speaker. The voice did nothing to belay the gruff impatience that set the tone at his office. *"You've reached Sawyer Construction. We're out of the office at the moment, but leave your name, number and a brief message, and we'll get back to you shortly. Wait for the beep."*

"Jack, it's Samantha. I read in the paper this morning that you've announced the start of construction on that shopping center." Not even the filtering of the tiny speaker on his machine could make her voice small. *"You know perfectly well the plans have not yet been approved by the Planning Commission. I'd advise you to call me the minute you get to your office."*

Cast of Characters

Miranda Jones: early 30s, 5'9, green eyes, long brunet hair, beautiful, lean, athletic; fine artist specializing in watercolors, acrylics and murals; a staunch environmentalist whose paintings often depict endangered species; has escaped her wealthy Bay-Area family to create a new life in Milford-Haven.

Will Marks: mid-30s, 6', dark eyes and hair, athletic build; VP at Clarke Shipping; contact of Zack Calvin's at Calvin Oil.

Randi Raines: early 30s, 5'5, black eyes, frosted hair, cute, athletic; demanding, impatient; a talk-show host in Los Angeles; dates Will Marks.

Samantha Hugo: early 50s, 5'9, cognac-brown eyes, redhead, statuesque, sharp dresser; Director of Milford-Haven's Environ-mental Planning Commission; Miranda's friend; Jack Sawyer's former wife; a journal writer.

Kevin Ransom: late-20s, 6'8, hazel eyes, sandy hair, strong jaw-line, lean, muscular; Foreman at Sawyer Construction; innocent, naive, kind; tuned in to animals; technologically adept; highly intuitive; has longings for Susan Winslow.

Jack Sawyer: mid-50s, 6', blue eyes, salt-and-pepper hair and mustache, barrel-chested, solidly muscular, ruggedly handsome; Milford-Haven contractor-builder; Samantha Hugo's former husband; secretly involved with Sally O'Mally.

Lucy Seecor: mid-30s, 5'6', black eyes, shiny black hair worn in a long braid; trim figure; photographic memory; manager of Rosencrantz Café.

Emily Wilkins: late 30s, 5'6, brown eyes, blond hair, Attractive and focused, soft-spoken but determined. Originally from South Africa, where her journalism career hit a stone wall with Apartheid, she moved to Milford-Haven and loves her new home as local journalist.

Mr. Cedric Worthington: mid-60s, 5'8, bald and with a stocky build; the kindly, longsuffering husband of "Mrs. Lime."

Mrs. Ezmeralda Worthington (AKA "Mrs. Lime"): mid-60s, 5'6, mousy brown hair and stocky build; a woman of firm, but not necessarily well-founded convictions, who nonetheless is always pleased to offer her advice and opinions.

COLOPHON

The print version of this book is set in the Cambria font, released in 2004 by Microsoft, as a formal, solid font to be equally readable in print and on screens. It was designed by Jelle Bosma, Steve Matteson, and Robin Nicholas.

The name Cambria is the classical name for Wales, the Latin form of the Welsh name for Wales, *Cymru*. The etymology of *Cymru* is *combrog,* meaning "compatriot."

The California town of Cambria is named for its resemblance to the south-western coast of Wales, where the town of Milford Haven has existed since before ancient Roman times, and is mentioned in William Shakespeare's *Cymbeline.*

The dingbat is the Mussel Shell, drawn by artist Mary Helsaple, and rendered graphically by designer Rebecca Finkel. The mussel is a bivalve marine creature that lives on exposed shores in the intertidal zones in California, Florida, the U.K., Japan, and on other beaches throughout the world. The shells, which are longer than they are wide, often with dark blue exteriors and silvery interiors, when open, resemble a pair of wings.

LIGHTHOUSE

Each of the *Milford-Haven Novels* features a real lighthouse, though in this book, the real one is used fictionally. The "Milford-Haven lighthouse" was designed and built, but never commissioned. In the story it exists as a restaurant.

The real Point Montara light was originally established in 1875 as a fog signal station. Although nearly 90 vessels had met with the business end of the jagged rocks off Montara by the mid-1800s, it wasn't until two high-profile incidents in 1868 and 1872 that Congress was finally propelled into action.

The first light at Point Montara was established in 1900, and consisted of a red lens-lantern hung on a post. A new fog signal building was built in 1902, and a fourth-order Fresnel lens was installed in 1912 on a skeleton tower. The light was electrified in 1919. Finally, in 1928, the current cast-iron, 30-foot tower was installed to house the Fresnel lens.

In 2008, it was discovered that the current Point Montara lighthouse is much older than previously thought. It was built in 1881 and erected on Wellfleet Harbor in Cape Cod, Massachusetts, where it stood until the light station was decommissioned in 1922. From Cape Cod, the lighthouse made a 3,000-mile journey to Yerba Buena Island in San Francisco Bay, where it waited in a depot until finally being installed at Point Montara in 1928. It is currently the only known lighthouse to have stood watch on two oceans.

Milford-Haven Recipes

Rosencrantz & Guildenstern Cafe
Apple Coleslaw

Ingredients: Serves 4-6

1.5 c	chopped green cabbage
1.5 c	chopped red cabbage
1	Unpeeled Granny Smith apple, cored & chopped
1	Unpeeled red apple, cored & chopped
1	Carrot, grated
2	green onions, finely chopped
1/3 c	mayonnaise
1/3 c	brown sugar
1 T	lemon juice

Preparation:

In a large bowl, combine green cabbage, red cabbage, red apple, green apple, carrot, and green onions.

In a small bowl, mix together mayonnaise, brown sugar and lemon juice.

Pour dressing over salad and mix well.

*Provided by Elaine Traxel Evans

Milford-Haven Recipes

"Cold Slob" Red Cabbage Slaw

Ingredients: serves 2 or more

1 head   shredded cabbage – red or white

½ cup   grated carrot

to taste   chopped walnuts

to taste   chopped onion — red or green

Dressing:

½ cup   vegenaise

1 t   tamari

1 t   balsamic vinegar

2 cloves   crushed garlic

Preparation:

In large bowl, toss together cabbage, carrots, onions, and walnuts.

 In a separate bowl, whisk together the ingredients for the dressing

Pour dressing over coleslaw. toss to mix well.

When Hummers Dream

Reading Group Topics for Discussion

1. This novelette differs from the novels in the series because it stands alone. How does it relate to the overall series? How does it differ? Do you prefer stories that have a traditional beginning, middle and end? Or do you prefer a serial story that continues through several books?

2. The story focuses on protagonist Miranda Jones, who lives in the world of art, and in the world of wildlife. How would you describe her relationship with the hummingbird in this novelette?

3. Do you believe animals have intelligence? Do you think the size of a physical brain determines the level of intelligence? Or can even small creatures "tap in" to a higher intelligence?

4. Have you had a special encounter with a wild creature? Share what that experience was like for you.

5. When "Mrs. Lime" arrives, she disparages Miranda's artistic ability, yet she has no art training herself. Do you feel she has every right to criticize someone else's work? Or do you feel she's the personification of obnoxious behavior?

6. When Mark brings his girlfriend to Milford-Haven, he expects to share with her a lovely time in a beautiful place. Yet she doesn't recognize the beauty and feels she's been cheated out of a weekend getaway. What kind of romantic getaway do you prefer? Something glamorous? Something rustic? Or something else entirely.

7. Though much of the story involves recognizable human behavior, the tale also includes an unusual perspective on a wildlife species. Would say this makes this a Paranormal novelette? What constitutes the paranormal for you?

8. How are the ideas of marriage and relationships expressed in this book? The older couple seem to be at odds, as does the younger. Do you believe relationships require work? Or should a true romance involve easy understanding and communication?

9. In addition to being a writer, Mara Purl is also an actress who spent a summer performing a play in the real town of Cambria, California. As both actor and writer, Mara studies people, yet this story includes an animal character. Is the hummer of equal interest and value as the people in her story?

10. Why is this book called *When Hummers Dream?* Do you believe the hummer truly dreamed? Does every creature dream? Or is its "dream" purely a figment of the author's imagination?

To share or print these discussion points please visit:
http://marapurl.com/books/when-hummers-dream/

Secret of the Shells

*Special Messages about a Woman and Her Self,
and about Discovering the Next Chapter . . . of Her Life*

 Shell: Mussel | ***When Hummers Dream***

• Do you have a sense of connection to animals? Do you feel you understand them? Do they understand you? Is this true both of pets and animals in the wild?

• What would you do if you were confronted by an animal you feared? Would you attempt to harm it? Outrun it? Or might you try holding in your thought a sense of respect for the animal?

• Do you believe animals have both waking and sleeping states of consciousness, much as we do?

• Have you ever imagined being able to "talk to the animals"? Have you ever watched videos of animal communicators? Do their efforts seem "made up" or authentic?

• Create animal communication experiments:

• Try holding sugar water in something red, to see whether a hummingbird might come to sip while you hold it.

• Go for a hike in a wild or semi-wild region. Try "addressing" the animal inhabitants with a "greeting" of respect. See if you glimpse any creatures as you walk. [Note: be prepared to make loud noise, carry walking sticks to make yourself "large", and consider carrying pepper spray as a backup safeguard.]

• View some of the videos posted by professional animal communicator Anna Breytenbach. Her work is awe inspiring.

To discover more about the Secrets of the Shells
visit www.MaraPurl.com.
To reach the author, by e-mail: MaraPurl@MaraPurl.com.
by mail: Mara Purl c/o Milford-Haven Enterprises
PO Box 7304-629
North Hollywood, CA 91603

Find yourself in . . .
Milford-Haven
Small town simplicities . . .
Global complexities . . .

"Where Jack, Zack, Miranda, Cornelius, Samantha, Rune, Meredith, Connie, Emily, Kevin, Joseph, Sally, Tony, Zelda, Notes, Susan, and Cynthia, are building, buying, painting, observing, planning, rehearsing, advising, traveling, reporting, cogitating, dominating, dishing, dealing, conniving, playing, sneaking, and seducing, respectively."

Subscribe to the Milford-Haven Podcast!
Enjoy the original BBC radio drama
with an all-star cast,
original music & sound effects,
plus Bonus Material!

Also available on CD or in downloadable formats
www.MilfordHaven.com

SALLY'S
WING DINGS
FINDERS

Mara Purl, author of the popular and critically acclaimed *Milford-Haven Novels,* pioneered small-town fiction for women.

Mara's beloved fictitious town has been delighting audiences since 1992, when it first appeared as *Milford-Haven, U.S.A.*©—the first American radio drama ever licensed and broadcast by the BBC. The show reached an audience of 4.5 million listeners in the U.K. In the U.S., it was the 1994 Finalist for the New York Festivals World's Best Radio Programs.

Mara was named the Top Female Author for Fiction by The Authors Show, and to date, her books have won more than forty book awards including the American Fiction, Benjamin Franklin, National Indie Excellence, USA Book News Best Books, and Fore-Word Books of the Year.

Mara's other writing credits include plays, screenplays, scripts for *Guiding Light,* cover stories for *Rolling Stone,* staff writing with the *Financial Times (of London),* and the Associated Press. She is the co-author (with Erin Gray) of *Act Right: A Manual for the On-Camera Actor.*

As an actress, Mara was "Darla Cook" on *Days Of Our Lives.* For the one-woman show *Mary Shelley: In Her Own Words*—which Mara performs and co-wrote (with Sydney Swire)—she earned a Peak Award, she has co-starred in multiple productions of *Sea Marks,* and plays the title role in *Becoming Julia Morgan.* She was named one of twelve Women of the Year by the Los Angeles County Commission for Women.

Mara is married to Dr. Larry Norfleet and lives in Los Angeles, and in Colorado Springs.

Visit her website at www.MaraPurl.com where you can subscribe to her newsletter and link to her social media sites. www.MaraPurl.WordPress.com. She welcomes e-mail from readers at MaraPurl@MaraPurl.com.

MARA PURL
Milford-Haven

Chronology at MaraPurl.com/Books